BREATHING
LIQUID

BREATHING LIQUID

LAUREN MIX

Copyright © 2021 by LM Editing

ISBN # 978-0-578-85738-1

Edited by Lauren Mix
LMEditingservices.com

LM Editing

Cover Design by Lauren Mix

Formatting by Kensington Type & Graphics
kentype.com

DEDICATION

Thank you to John for giving me an opportunity all those years ago; to my mom for reading each draft and providing valuable feedback; and to my husband, Patrick, for supporting and encouraging me every step of the way. – **Lauren**

June 27, 2019

Maynard Children's Hospital housed its personnel in a physical hierarchy. Whether this was intentional or coincidental was undetermined. The administrative staff was located on the third floor, above the emergency room and the radiology and pathology departments. Mid-level leadership was aptly situated on the 6th floor, equally spaced between the administration offices and executive management. Of course, each department also had offices distributed around their respective floors for the shift leads and whatnot, which slightly veiled the blatant grading, but the intent of this effect was also uncertain.

The Chair of Pediatrics had the fourth of seven offices on the 6th floor, a location that he chose to consider as purposeful, right smack in the middle of it all. No, it wasn't a coveted corner office, nor was it the largest in the hall. But, from his window, he could see past the parking lot and interstate to the river that cupped the bustling downtown area, and he was equally spaced between the elevators and bathrooms.

His desk phone, a relic amidst the modern technology scattered throughout his office, rang loudly as he tidied the space around it.

"Hello?" Jay said into the receiver.

"Hi, Dr. Greenspan. This is Mary Archer, executive assistant to Walter Trush. He asked me to reach out to you to confirm the personal cell phone number listed in your file, so I can arrange a meeting for the two of you next Monday."

"Oh, umm sure. It's 513-993-0306," Jay replied, caught off-guard by the request, but before he could say anything else, Mary continued.

"Thank you. Walter will be in town next week and would like to meet with you for dinner this coming Monday. I will text you the exact time and location once I've confirmed reservations. He asks that this meeting remain confidential. Please do not include it on your calendar, reference it in any way in email or mention it to anyone." Her tone was cold and crisp, freezing Jay in place. "Thank you, Dr. Greenspan. I'll be in touch," she informed and disconnected the call.

What the hell was that about? Jay thought. *Did I somehow fall into a different reality where I am no longer Department Chair of Pediatrics and am now some sort of spy?* He chuckled to himself before giving it more thought. He quickly considered the potential agendas for the meeting and realized that several carried a weight that wasn't something to scoff at.

He stood at his desk, computing the possibilities, the phone like an anchor in his hand, holding him in place, its cord shorter than he recalled. Several of the options were concerning, one was exciting. *Could it be?* he wondered. The thought produced another chuckle, and he returned the phone to its cradle, shrugging off the idea and the exchange. He then resumed gathering his belongings to head home after another long day.

Traffic was surprisingly light, so he made good time. Jay

climbed the deck stairs to the side door that had, over the years, become the main entry and exit point of his house, funneling the family in and out by way of the kitchen. The front door served its purpose for guests and deliveries when it wasn't providing aesthetics. Inside, Kathy was seated at the kitchen table with her half-eaten dinner, a nearly empty glass of wine and a full plate set across from hers, waiting for him. He leaned in and kissed her cheek. She smiled an exhausted smile that only a fellow physician could fully appreciate and interpret as meaning she'd had a busy but successful day at work, which, in her case, was in the emergency room.

Jay dropped his stuff into its usual spot by the counter and settled in across the table from Kathy. "You'll never guess what phone call I got today. I think it might actually happen." He blushed, still marginally perplexed by Mary's call. "A dinner meeting is being set up for Monday."

Kathy's eyes awoke with interest. "Really? That's great!" Her smile was quickly replaced with hesitation. "You're going to rehearse the different outcome scenarios, so you're prepared this time, right? I know how much you like to wing these types of things, but I think you owe it to yourself to plan for this one." She bit the inside of her lip in an unconscious effort to temper her sudden yet anxious excitement. She wanted this so badly for Jay. He deserved it, after all. "There's a lot to consider and even more at stake."

Jay looked at his wife, chewing her lip in the cute way she had of trying to disguise her worry. She was always so cautious about the things that excited her and their potential to come into grasp only to be whisked away. It's one of the traits that made her an outstanding ER physician – she never got too comfortable and always thought ahead.

"Don't worry, Kath. You know I always land on my feet." He flashed her a grin. "But yes, I'll talk through the various possibilities and appropriate responses. I already left Mark a voicemail, asking to do exactly that."

Mark, owner of a successful leadership consulting firm, had been hired to guide the Maynard Children's Hospital's organizational transformation back in 2006. The two men had since become friends. In fact, Mark's leadership principles and processes had so thoroughly impressed Jay that he rarely approached any work situation these days without consulting Mark first.

"Oh good. He always gives such sound advice. I just hope you actually follow it." Kathy sighed and gave him a lighthearted eyeroll. "Now, eat. That steak won't be near as good reheated."

***

Ding! Ding! Jay's personal phone chirped as he walked down the hallway towards his office. He was in a particularly good mood for a Monday, ready for the day, the evening, and the week. Retrieving his phone from his pocket, he saw that the message was from a hospital number, unsaved in his contacts. *Must be from Mary then*, he assumed and slid his finger up the screen, unlocking it to read the text.

> Good morning. Please meet Dr. Walter Trush at O6OO at D'Marina on River Road. Please confirm receipt.

Cool. At least I'll enjoy the food, thought Jay, double-tapping Mary's message to "like it" as confirmation before returning the phone to his pocket. He turned into his office, tossing his stuff onto the chair by the door as he always did and got right to work.

Jay didn't have time to think about his upcoming meeting again for the rest of the day, which was probably for the best. Maybe Walter planned to offer him his dream job. Maybe Walter simply intended to discuss a restructure that would affect enough of the leadership that it had to remain hush-hush until being announced. Maybe he would be part of it, and Walter was going to fire him. Maybe he'd be asked to raid the lost ark.

Whatever this clandestine meeting was about, he'd take it in stride, just as he did with everything else. Plus, he'd thought about this moment enough in his lifetime, and he and Mark had prepared for a variety of potential scenarios and suitable responses. No stone had been left unturned, no possibility unassessed.

Mark had strongly recommended that, in the event of an offer, he be gracious and tempered with his reply, which should include the request for a short amount of time to think it over. Then, after a day or so of consideration, Jay would return with conditional acceptance. Mark had explicitly said *not* to immediately accept anything, dream job or not.

While Mark stressed the importance of maintaining leverage for negotiations, Kathy worried about Jay getting his hopes up too high. All that mattered to Jay was that he might finally be given a chance. Before heading into work, he had reassured both Mark and Kathy that he would 'stick to the script,' but none of the three had much confidence in that.

***

The restaurant's parking lot was lightly peppered with vehicles, offering plenty of open spaces. Not wanting to seem obvious, Jay quickly scanned for Walter's car as he selected a spot off to the side by a small cluster of cars that he assumed belonged to the staff.

D'Marina's varied slightly from other kitschy Italian restaurants. It had the staples; grapevine wallpaper, curtains with wine glasses and bottles on them, olive oil pourers on each table, and Frank Sinatra on the stereo. But, unlike its typical counterparts, the kitchen was set up as an intentional part of the atmosphere, with low half-walls dividing the space, allowing a full view of the bread being baked, pasta being rolled, salads being tossed. On crowded nights, the sounds from the kitchen mingled with those from the dining room, creating an acoustical tango of talk and taste.

He'd arrived early, hoping to get himself situated ahead of time but, upon entering, found that Walter had done the same. Jay pointed to Walter as the young hostess greeted him. "Oh yes. Follow me," she said, grabbing a menu. She led him across the large room full of empty tables to where Walter sat finishing the last drops of a beer. Jay felt the eyes of every server and cook, unoccupied from the lack of customers, watch him shake Walter's hand and join him at the table that was far too large for only the two men.

"Thank you for meeting with me," Walter said as Jay sat down.

"No problem at all. Thank you for making the time," Jay replied while he cleared his table settings to the side and took the menu from the hostess.

"I'll have another," Walter informed the young girl who hadn't been prepared to take any orders.

"Oh...Ok—" she began.

"It was the lager on tap," Walter added, thinking it would resolve the expression on her face.

"I'll have the same, please," Jay said, trying to make it easy for her.

"Umm, I'm just the hostess. I can't take orders, but I will tell your waitress that you would like two more lagers," she nervously managed to reply.

"Oh yes, my apologies. Please do inform her. Thank you," Walter answered, verbally shooing her away.

She scurried over to their waitress, who was busy flirting with the pizza chef, to relay the order while Walter gave Jay some time to review the menu. Jay was thankful for a break after the awkward trek across the dining room and mix-up with the hostess who had done as she'd said because their waitress was already headed to their table with two pints of lager.

In a cordial attempt to familiarize and lighten the tension, the two men made small talk. They had worked together for no longer than 9 months and had only met twice, briefly. They knew little about one another outside of their individual responsibilities.

As the new CEO of Penmarche, the parent institution to both Maynard Children's and Sherman University hospitals, Walter oversaw all three and their CEOs from Penmarche's main facility in Texas. Not known for his personal approach, his small yet muscular frame and serious expression matched his management style to a certain degree. He wasn't a typical pediatric surgeon. Despite being accustomed to making quick decisions in the operating room, he was surprisingly cautious outside of it. Yet, true to his vocation, he was precise and very strategic in his decision-making.

Walter's platform had remained consistent since his first day; transition healthcare from being paid to treat the sick to being paid to keep children healthy. Although this was a national desire, he was tired of the stagnant progress and used his position to push the agenda forward by empowering others and hiring consultants to increase the organization's philanthropy. However, he did most of this from behind the scenes, making few actual decisions on his own and saying even less when he visited each ward.

Despite their intent, the conversation remained focused on surface items in the same way it does when coworkers find themselves on a conference call before everyone else has joined. It didn't take long for Walter to find it a pointless exercise. Not halfway into their beers, he got straight to the point, explaining the purpose of their meeting, reason for its secrecy, and hope for its outcome.

"What happens at the end? Would everything just go back to normal?" Jay asked, unpacking the questions brewing in his head.

"Well, we don't exactly have a plan for after, but we will, of course, have to fill your current role once you step into the new one. I will make sure you're taken care of though. Don't worry about that part of the equation," Walter assured, seemingly brushing off Jay's concerns.

The coupling of his short tenure at Maynard and his unconventional management style didn't exactly motivate Jay to trust him. But, with his mission being to help more children, Jay figured he'd at least hear him out.

"Wow. OK. This is a lot to process..." Jay paused, rubbing the back of his neck, and tried to organize the ideas that were crowding the many questions he had. Despite rehearsing this conversation with Mark, he found himself forgetting his lines. "When you say 'interim', how exactly do you define that?"

Walter looked at Jay and briefly considered his answer before responding. "10 months. That's how long we assume it will take to find the right candidate and complete the hiring process. We're looking for a fresh perspective and, thus, intend to search externally to fill this role, which is why you will not be considered. I'm sure you understand..." Walter trailed off because he knew that Jay was an ideal candidate for the Maynard CEO role and didn't want to be pushed for further explanation. He wasn't sure he could expand on the reasoning for an external search.

Walter knew that Jay was, what some would call, a triple threat physician. After 30 years of practicing neonatology (a hospital-based subspecialty of pediatrics that consists of the medical care of newborn infants, especially the ill or premature newborn), he had established himself as a great clinician and educator with a solid career in research under his belt. He knew how to care for patients and carried himself with a calm sense of confidence and concern. Even after 15 years as Chairman of the Department of Pediatrics for Maynard Children's Hospital he remained grounded and was viewed positively throughout his ward by his staff and patient families.

"While we conduct our search, I want you to concentrate on the role and not worry about the 'politics' of it," Walter advised. "With the success in your current role and your knowledge of our system and complex, evolving environment, we know you'll do a great job."

Walter cut a bite of the veal he'd ordered, and Jay pushed the spinach off his shrimp and moved it around his plate, distorting the Florentine element of the dish, while he absorbed the numerous facets contained in Walter's few words.

Walter isn't wrong about me, he thought. *This move makes sense, even if it is only temporary.* Jay pictured the changes and progress he'd envisioned finally taking place, feeling the excitement rise to the surface.

He'd imagined this opportunity so many times. After all, this was his dream job, his way to enact the change he knew was needed to take the organization to the next level. What was there to really think about? But he knew he couldn't immediately accept. The script dictated otherwise. However, he hadn't anticipated a scenario where, afterwards, he would have no defined plan or chance at the permanent position.

It's not every day you get the opportunity to explore your dream job though! He swallowed a perfectly cooked cherry tomato and the temporary portion of the offer then blurted, "Walter, I know I should negotiate terms and conditions." He hesitated and straightened himself in his seat. "But it would be an honor to be the interim CEO. I know I'll do a good job. The only thing you'll regret will be not considering me for the permanent role." Jay beamed beneath his uncontained excitement though, he immediately wondered if he should have forced himself to sit on this for a day, as Mark had advised.

He knew he had a tendency of leaping at opportunities before he'd had time to really think them through. He attributed this characteristic, in part, to having watched his father navigate life in a responsible yet largely carefree manner. Jay's father had been determined to trade in his boring childhood for fun, accepting any challenge presented and preferring activities that were typically accompanied with a shot of adrenaline.

Along with an unfiltered sense of humor and willingness to push social limits – sometimes consciously, sometimes not – Jay shared this penchant for risk, which manifested itself in a variety of ways, from his approach with different opportunities to selecting a career as a neonatologist. Regardless of the reasoning, he was fully aware of the fact that he trusted too easily and too quickly at times. However, since this mentality had largely worked out well to date for Jay, he saw no reason to change the course.

He figured Mark would understand his deviation from the script, knowing that money was not his driver. So, he raised his glass to Walter and the opportunity, embracing his decision, and finished the last sip of beer.

Walter returned the gesture. "Thank you, Jay. I know you'll do a great job." He paused over the brim of his beer glass, adding, "Please don't mention anything to anyone until we make the official announcement next week. Your discretion is much appreciated."

"Well, can I at least tell my wife, Kathy?"

"As long as you trust her," Walter remarked without changing his familiar gruff expression.

Jay smirked to himself, unsure whether Walter was kidding. But it didn't matter. He was just offered his dream job! The remainder of the meal was a blur of formalities and pleasantries. He could not wait to call Kathy!

No one watched as they walked across the restaurant to leave. Jay noticed that its increased patronage had refocused the staff. He thanked Walter, once again, for trusting him with this responsibility and the meal then restrained himself from sprinting to his car. Once inside, he sat behind the wheel, replaying the whole scene.

So what if it has to be kept a secret for the moment! And so what if it is only temporary! Some people go their whole lives never coming within grasp of their dreams. What am I supposed to do, turn the offer down because I'm only to be a placeholder? He laughed at his thoughts because he knew himself well enough to know that he would not waste this opportunity. That simply wasn't the way he operated.

Jay saw this as his moment to shine, to make essential changes to the current system, process, and policies. He would prove he deserved this role. He'd take whatever time he had to accomplish as much as he could. *Isn't that how anyone would approach this situation? Wouldn't anyone see this as an opportunity rather than a slight and use this chance to improve their organization?*

In the grand scheme of things, ten months isn't much time…for anything enjoyable, that is. It is, however, certainly long enough to make an impact, which was exactly what Jay was determined to do. He planned to take everything he'd learned to date – every piece of advice received, every decision made, every step taken, every 'yes' exclaimed – and use it to better the organization for the future.

Jay dropped his phone into the vacant cupholder in the center console and drove home with his thoughts churning, pride swelling, and excitement overflowing. This was way too important to tell Kathy over the phone! He wanted to see the look on her face.

PART ONE

Getting to the Dinner Table

Botany & the Undergrad

Jay had been a mediocre student at his high school outside of Cincinnati, much more interested in sports than academics. Though there wasn't much they agreed on those days, his parents both expected him to continue onto college, which left Jay faced with the decision of *where*, not *if*, he would go.

In order to check off the "go to college" box, Jay selected and attended Connecticut College, a small liberal arts institution on the coast of New England, where he found the laid-back nature of the classes motivating and surprisingly enjoyable. In a short time, he acquired a fondness for studying and began to take pride in his good grades.

Between classes and dorm life, Jay established a fun group of friends that both complemented and encouraged his academic success. They met regularly to study in the arboretum, a large, wooded area adjacent to campus, and equally as often to unwind at the campus bar on dollar beer nights. Jay's daily routine developed into an ideal balance of friends, academics, and freedom.

As his academic confidence was building, so, too, was

the pressure to decide on a major. Up until this point, Jay had been enjoying the freedoms that came with being away at college, simply going through the motions without much thought of formulating a plan for what came after. He was content in his routine – study, socialize, test, repeat.

Consistent with his technique to date, Jay had half-heartedly committed to studying botany after briefly factoring in the college's well-respected program and his interest in plants, including the recreational kind (it being the 70s and all). There wasn't much more strategy or substance to the decision beyond that. Jay was comfortable and felt no need to adjust focus. It was quite simple; botany meant science and science meant Jay was interested.

Unintentionally, this decision played out well for him as the college was small and its science courses not very competitive. He had yet to find himself under the intense pressure experienced by those at the larger, more cut-throat universities, wondering if he or any of the other students would pass and return next semester. With the exception of Physics, Jay breezed through his courses with an ordinary amount of effort.

In the fall of his junior year, the leaves began to change, and the air became crisp. He was genuinely satisfied with the comfortable notch he'd carved out for himself within university life, which consisted of a respectable GPA and solid group of friends with a healthy social life. Even as the time for next semester's course selection arrived, he continued on in his turbulence-free routine.

Walking across campus towards his appointment with his botany professorial advisor, he blended in with the other students in stride, many of which were under-dressed for the weather, as college students tended to be. The wind swirled the leaves around his flip-flops, encouraging a quicker pace as he navigated on autopilot to the building that housed the science department.

He stepped inside the building and made his way to the 3rd floor, thankful for the warmth of the radiators lining the halls. Dr. Plant's office door was ajar, welcoming him into the familiar space. Jay had spent plenty of time discussing course projects seated amongst the numerous florae in various stages of growth, stacks of lab sheets, and large inventory of books, some shelved, some not. The small, one-window office offered a palliative embrace to the students who entered. Furthermore, he enjoyed Dr. Plant's company and considered him a steady, positive influence in his academic life.

"Jay, what are you going to do when all of this is over?" Dr. Plant looked up from the catalog they were perusing to select next semester's courses. Jay, reading the description of an organic chemistry course, shrugged in response. Dr. Plant persisted. "I'm serious, Jay. Have you given any thought into how you will apply a botany degree in the real world?"

Jay's initial reaction was to laugh off the question, but upon seeing the intensity in Dr. Plant's face, quickly realized that it was not asked in passing. He closed his copy of the catalog, keeping his index finger in the page where he'd left off, and considered this. He had not anticipated the conversation moving beyond next semester, having not thought that far ahead yet. Truthfully, he didn't know what he would do 'in the real world'. However, he did know that moving home would not be an option, so he'd most certainly need a decent job.

"I've been thinking about becoming a researcher," he

lied. It sounded good enough, and he assumed it sufficed as a safe answer to give a college advisor. Jay waited for him to react, expecting him to be pleased with this direction but, instead, was met with a seriousness he had never seen in Dr. Plant. "Or maybe a forest ranger!" he quickly added, hoping this would resolve Dr. Plant's somber expression.

"Jay, don't be an idiot..." Dr. Plant sighed in exasperation, shaking his head ever so slightly. "You enjoy science, and you're clearly good at it. Become a doctor. You can always do research, but this way you can also make some money..." He suggested this without breaking eye contact. "And, if the forest still calls you, you'll be able to afford trips to the national parks." There was something in his intense, almost urgent tone that made this advice seem more like a plea, even after the added quip.

What does he know? What does he see in me? wondered Jay, who hadn't considered anything beyond the title much less the profitability of a career in research or forestry.

Dr. Plant's gaze shifted to somewhere off in the distance while Jay sat across from him stunned by the question, contemplating the idea of becoming Dr. Jay Greenspan, MD.

"Yeah, ok...I think I could do that," he mused as a smile emerged on his face. "Yeah," he repeated, more to himself than to Dr. Plant.

Several moments passed while both men absorbed the weight of this decision. Jay nodded in agreement with the subsequent stream of thoughts about his newly found direction. "I think I will like it, too."

Jay later realized that Dr. Plant, although seemingly happy, had relived his own decisions and regret through Jay in that moment. Jay would never know what impact, if any at all, that discussion had on Dr. Plant, but for him, it forged the path to, what would become, a solid and satisfying career as a physician. It also marked the first of many 'yes moments' that would pave the way to greater things. Years later, Jay would look back on this as the defining moment of a common theme in his life – trusting given advice and making snap decisions to better himself and the lives of many, many families.

2

Medical School & Formulation of a Plan

Jay rubbed his eyes with the palms of his hands and struggled to stay awake. He had 40 more pages to study for his Chemistry test the next day and couldn't afford to tire out now. Although he was still earning good grades, school was no longer the carefree balance of studying, socializing and freedom. Gone were the days of studying for an hour or so before meeting up with the guys for a beer. Those had been replaced with the funneling of as much new information into his head as possible in an amount of time that seemed unreasonably short.

The breakneck speed of course material overwhelmed him. He showed up to his first day of classes at Case Western University expecting to receive his syllabus and required textbook list, go through the introductions of students to professor, learn the goals and expectations of the course then be dismissed to prepare for the learning that would begin next time. Instead, the full class duration was spent reviewing material that took a month to learn as an undergrad at Connecticut College.

It became extremely and suddenly obvious to Jay that he had no clue what he'd signed himself up for. Come to think of it, had Dr. Plant, a *botany* professor, even known what to expect? It was only then that Jay realized he should have explored, even minimally, the suggestion he'd said yes to in the familiar office on that brisk fall day in Connecticut. Perhaps, approaching a major life decision with an element of caution was a good idea. Hindsight was 20/20, as is often the case, but Jay was no quitter. Owning his decision, he remained focused and managed to survive the first 2 years of medical school without whiplash. Of course, it didn't hurt that the prettiest girl at the university (and in all of Cleveland, if you asked Jay), Kathy Nasci, was in his class.

He jumped on every opportunity to ask her to study together, and although she often accepted the invitations, he knew he didn't stand a chance at anything outside of their study group. Nevertheless, Jay was happy just to be with her, even if it was only for academic reasons.

One evening, as the last remaining light from the sun ducked behind the tree line and, one by one, the lights scattered throughout campus came to life, he stood outside Kathy's dormitory, waiting for her to join him for their study session at the library. They had a milestone test at the end of the week, covering most of the material to date. This was no time to become unfocused, but Jay couldn't help it.

She walked out with her messenger bag draped over her slender shoulder. The contrast of her small frame saddled with the bulky course material in her bag made him wonder how she was even remaining upright under its weight. He joined her stride towards their destination. The breeze was light but strong enough to carry the scent of honeysuckle from her hair to his nose. They chatted effortlessly along the path, and Jay could think of no place he'd rather be. *Maybe medical school isn't so bad after all,* he thought.

***

As he progressed into the third year, he found there was more to the program than cramming knowledge into his brain and absorbing as much new information as possible. He had advanced into the next phase – rotating through hospitals – which better suited Jay's extroverted personality. He enjoyed meeting and talking to people, and the residents, attendings, nurses and patients gave him plenty of opportunities. Though he found the book learning difficult to translate into helping an actual patient, the listening part came easy. Jay enjoyed visiting with patients, listening to their stories, and sharing experiences. He was building confidence and relationships, which helped him with the challenges of applying the physiology to aid in diagnosing and treating. He was learning to love medicine.

"Good evening," Jay said as he handed laboratory results to a member of the medical team. When he wasn't on rotation, Jay made himself available to assist in a variety of ways purely because he enjoyed helping people, whether they be doctor or patient. He wasn't above getting ice for someone with a dry mouth or listening to a patient tell a story to pass the time or allaying the concerns of worried family members. He simply liked being part of a healing process.

"How are things, Doug?" Jay asked, poking his head into one of the rooms on his way down the hall.

"Eh, I'm laying here, talking to you, so I could be better, I suppose," the 46-year-old recovering from a minor stroke wryly replied.

"Ah yes, but it could be worse too, right?" Jay countered with a friendly smirk. He'd moved fully into the room now. "Is there anything new going on that's making you more pessimistic than usual today?"

Doug scoffed at Jay, who had taken a seat in the visitor's chair. "Aren't you on your way out? You came in here before I even got breakfast this morning! Don't they let you go home at some point?!" Doug forced a smile to his face but lacked nonchalance in his eyes.

"I'm headed that direction now but wanted to check in with you since I was passing by. So, I'll ask again. Is there anything new going on that's making you extra pessimistic today? Outside of your apparent hearing loss, that is?"

This time, Doug's smile was genuine as he shifted his gaze down. "Ya know, I just can't help beating myself up for being in here. It's not like we all don't know that smoking and being over-weight aren't a healthy combination. I just didn't think it'd happen to me, is all," Doug confessed.

Jay knew that, although Doug was on the mend, his chances of effectively losing weight and quitting smoking were slim. And despite everyone's best efforts, he would likely be back again. The adults in the ward seemingly had some self-destructive behavior, from drug abuse to smoking, and medicine could not hold back time. These behaviors always caught up with them.

"Well, if I had a dollar for every time someone said that to me, I'd be a very rich man." He turned in his chair to face Doug. "Listen, you can't let that get to you. What's done is done, and you were lucky this time. You should fully recover, barring anything wildly outside the statistics. It's what you do from here on out that matters," Jay encouraged, not fully believing his own words.

"I have two kids, Doc. I am, by no means, the world's best dad, but I love them. I can't stand thinking about the worry this is causing them and my wife," admitted Doug.

Jay stood up and removed Doug's chart from its holder. After reviewing the notes from today he said, "Alright, well it says here you'll be discharged sometime this week. Instead of harping on what you did or didn't do right that landed you in here, why not formulate your plan for moving forward? Think about how you can change your diet in a way that will last. I'm sure there are sports you could get involved in with your kids. If not, start a new routine where you all exercise regularly together in some way. Not only is that healthier, it'll bring you all closer while also establishing healthy habits for your children."

"Yeah, you make a good point, Doc. I really do need to start thinking about that kind of stuff." He paused for a moment then continued. "How long have you been at this? You can't be but a kid yourself, yet you're already a damn good doctor. I wish they all took the time that you do. It helps."

"Thanks," Jay flushed, humbled by the kind words. "I'm nowhere near the end or even middle of my journey as a physician, but I can tell you that I'm enjoying it so far. Talking with patients like you helps keep me grounded in the humanity of the practice. Over time, far too many physicians lose sight of the actual patient, focusing only on the illness or injury."

"Ain't that the truth! My own doctor doesn't even stop in as frequently as you! But these nurses...they can't seem to leave me alone! Is it too much to ask to sleep for more than an hour at a time in here?!" Doug laughed, exasperated.

"Well, I'll leave you to it, then," saluted Jay, standing to leave. "But I'll be sure to check on you tomorrow on my way in. And seriously, don't ever forget that you were lucky this time. Make that count. As much as I enjoy our chats in here, I think we both would prefer to be having them over a beer somewhere, huh?" He moved towards the door to leave.

"Amen to that, Doc. Have a good one, and thanks for stopping in. I guess I'll see ya tomorrow then." Doug gave a wave then fumbled with the TV remote, eventually tuning into a Gilligan's Island rerun.

Jay rapped the doorframe before continuing down the hall towards the exit. He made three more stops to the three remaining rooms along the way before actually leaving.

Jay's capacity to love and being unafraid to show it was something he'd learned from his father, who had spent time teaching his children the importance of being genuine, claiming that it not only strengthened relationships but also tapered expectations.

Early on, Jay was taught that he could only control his own actions and behavior and that no amount of effort would affect unwanted change in another. In other words, to see the change, he had to be the change or else just move on.

Amongst this advice, his father had also offered other pearls of wisdom that weren't as obvious or pertinent to daily life and likely due to him being a Freudian psychiatrist, such as to think with the head on his shoulders and never to make a decision during certain "intimate" activities. Nevertheless, Jay unexpectedly found every bit of his instruction applicable at one point or another.

Fortunately, his father's brazen approach was tempered

by the calmer demeanor of his mother, who saw life through
the lens of an occupational therapist, and the impact of the
two was more balanced in their children.

By the time Jay had reached this point in his life, he had
woven his father's teachings and mother's equanimity into
his behavior, practicing them regularly and rather subcon-
sciously, which distinguished him from many of his peers.
He popped in to say hello or make small talk with as many
patients as he could on each shift, for both his and their
benefit. It kept him grounded and approachable.

These visits were easy compared to those he made while
on pediatric rotation. Adult patients were likely to make
full recoveries from their 'self-inflicted' wounds, at least the
first time around. Jay realized the contrasting innocence of
children during his first day on pediatric rotation where he
was assigned to a little girl with a brain tumor. She wasn't
ill from smoking or drinking or some other vice. It was
because of this innocence that he felt a greater sense of
meaning and accomplishment when interacting with the
pediatric patients. This was his calling, and discovering his
purpose dulled the pain from the endless hours with his
face in a book.

***

As medical school wound down, Jay would not repeat
the scenario in Dr. Plant's office. This time, he did not need
any advice or counsel on his next steps. He knew exactly
what he planned to do; become an intern then a resident
in pediatrics. He believed this synced perfectly with his
unfolding mission to heal and make a difference.

Jay found it inspiring to be alongside parents, often
close to his own age, who were fully committed to and

engaged in the care of their child. Of course, every parent wants what is best for their child, so they are compliant with directions and fully present while interacting with the medical team. Jay became aware of just how resilient children really were during his time in medical school. Unlike their older counterparts, pediatric patients were able to heal from even the direst of circumstances.

Jay sat at the desk in his apartment, answering the seemingly endless questions on the application for residency.

"Ya know? If you'd have told me five years ago, while I met with my Botany advisor, that I would be applying for residency at St. Raphael's Hospital for Children, I would have thought you were high!" Jay regarded, laughing in disbelief at the evolution of his academic career.

"Well, five years ago, *you* probably *were* high!" answered Kathy, who was studying on his couch in what had become a more frequent occurrence as their friendship grew. Jay acknowledged her good point and continued to contemplate that sentinel meeting with Dr. Plant.

Many uncertainties surrounded his decision to pursue medicine, but the one that he truly could not provide a definitive answer for was, *what if he hadn't simply said 'yes'?* He often wondered if he'd have navigated to pediatrics or even medicine had it not been suggested to him. Research was no longer a blip on his radar screen. *Had Dr. Plant known that the interest would fade away?*

During his first two years of intense learning and studying he had hated that 'yes'. But now, he'd come to be grateful for it. That 'yes' had given him a purpose and direction that he was excited to fulfill! If he could pull a child through an illness, his 'yes' could have a return of 100 years of health for that individual. Plus, that 'yes' had also led him to Kathy, who hovered just out of his reach, like a word on the tip of his tongue.

He wasn't sure why, but somehow, having her quiz him on course material, along with the use of other various study methods, increased his retention exponentially. Perhaps it was the soft tone of her voice or the flicker of possibility in her eyes that turned her into a living mnemonic. Whatever it was, it worked. He absorbed her words like a plant being watered after a drought, reinforcing his appreciation for the 'yes' that led him away from botany and into medicine.

**

After a particularly busy shift, Jay entered the diner with a plan to devour one, possibly even two, Big Guy Platters. While waiting to be seated by someone in the understaffed restaurant, he noticed Kathy sitting at a table, picking at her plate with a somber expression.

"Mind if I join you?" he asked as he went to slide into the opposing side of the booth.

She startled out of her haze and looked up at the interruption. "Oh, hi…No, I don't mind at all," she replied still preoccupied. As she began clearing the table space in front of him, out of the corner of his eye, he caught her quickly try to tame the commotion of curls that framed her face. He wondered if they smelled of honeysuckle.

"How are you? You seem like you're somewhere else," he remarked.

"No, I'm here," she scoffed weakly. "Just a rough day in the ER, is all."

He grimaced, knowing that a rough day in the emergency room could mean any number of tragic events.

"Well, tell me about it. What happened?" he asked with concern, folding his hands on the table in front of him.

She brushed the suggestion out of the air. "I'm sure the last thing you want to do after a long day is listen to more 'shop talk'."

"Try me," he prodded gently.

"Are you sure?"

"As I'll ever be. So come on, talk. Tell me what's got you so troubled and spare me no details."

She hesitated, resting her forehead in the palm of her hand in defeat, and filled Jay in. "We had a guy brought in from a car accident today…" She sighed heavily. "I just don't know what it will take to convince people to wear their seatbelts. So many lives would be saved, so many injuries less severe. I mean, when I tell you this guy's face was broken, I mean it was BRO-KEN! It was like the steering wheel had pushed his nose to the back of his head, Jay…It was so awful…and heartbreaking…" she trailed off and looked up with tired eyes at him.

The couple seated behind her turned and glared at them with disgusted looks on their faces. Jay saw the man at the table beside them noticeably pause before taking the bite he carried towards his mouth.

Jay smiled at her.

"What?" she asked, becoming defensive. "You asked!"

"No, no. Nothing's wrong on my end, but maybe we should move this recap to a location that doesn't involve people eating nearby," he mock-whispered, shrugging his shoulders and nodding towards the tables around them.

She followed his eyes and cringed. "I guess I forget that not everyone is used to hearing that kind of talk."

"Good thing I'm not 'everyone', but for the sake of

others…" Jay searched for a way to validate her feelings before changing the subject to something lighter. He related to the overwhelming emotional pendulum that accompanied working with real patients that could not be appreciated when they were just studying the scenarios in books. It was hard to see people in pain, in fear for their own or a family member's well-being; especially when something as simple as wearing a seatbelt could have prevented it.

"If only people didn't think of themselves as exceptions to the rule or statistics, right? However, I plan to use that exact mentality on what I order to eat and ignore the calorie count!" Jay paused momentarily while he calculated the risk of laying his cards on the table. "In fact, the only thing sweeter than the brownie sundae I plan to inhale is being here with you. I can't think of a single thing I'd rather do at the end of a day than sit and talk with you about anything." She blushed and tucked the curls behind her ears.

They stayed in that booth for a while, absorbed in conversation that didn't end with the topic of medicine. Afterwards, Jay walked Kathy back to her dorm where he took another gamble by leaning in to kiss her. She met him halfway and reciprocated the sentiment. Her lips were soft and her hair, untamed in the breeze, danced around their faces, trailing whispers of honeysuckle in the air. When they parted, he opened the door for her, his head still buzzing from his wager's payout. She smiled and ducked inside after saying goodnight. He smiled back and promised to call her later.

After she'd disappeared into the dorm elevator, he turned and began the walk back to his apartment, replaying the evening over in his head.

Although Jay's first two years in Cleveland had failed to produce an interest in the city or any of its female residents, his third year ushered in a newfound appeal. This was, in part, due to the shift away from the monotony and intensity of 'textbook education' to a more balanced oscillation between studying and tending to real patients. It was also attributable to the fact that he and Kathy had started dating.

Kathy energized the already lively 20-something Jay, complementing his life in a way he never thought possible. On their rare, coinciding days off, they explored the city, searching for things two people steeped in student loan debt could do. They enjoyed the challenge of finding meal specials and inexpensive entertainment. Jay felt so lucky to have found (and 'caught') a girl like Kathy. The icing on the cake was that she, too, felt it was her mission to heal, which she planned to do with her focus in internal medicine. They were a perfect match.

***

"Would you please stop worrying?!" Kathy rolled her eyes and sighed in the passenger seat of Jay's rickety, white 1979 Chevy Chevette.

"I'm not *worried*. But you can't tell me it's not intimidating for a lone Jewish kid to walk into a room filled with Italian-Catholics…that are your brothers! I mean, c'mon, Kath, I'm dating their baby sister. They might pummel me!" Jay said, only half-kidding.

"OK, but they won't. I'm telling you, if they don't like you, they'll love you simply because *I* love you," she assured him and gave his hand a squeeze. "Just put a filter on that Greenspan mouth of yours, and everything will be ok!" she joked. She'd recognized many similarities between

Jay and his father, one of the most prominent being the lack of conversational limits that sometimes bordered on awkwardness, especially when placed in an uncomfortable situation.

Jay made a motion as if he were zipping his lips and pretended to relax by turning the radio up. He focused on the three years of medical school behind him, the summer at home in Cincinnati ahead of him, and the girl of his dreams beside him. And if Kathy's brothers were to be the end of him, he would die a happy man.

Though, as it turned out, they didn't try to kill or even pummel him. In fact, her whole family was one of the kindest, most normal families he'd ever met. For this, he was thankful, since his own family hadn't been a whole family, at least not in the same room, since he was a teenager. He liked going to Kathy's parents' house, if only to get a semblance of 'normal'.

Once again, Jay's gratitude for the many 'yes moments' that had gotten him to this point bubbled to the surface. He still wasn't sure if he'd have ever found this path without Dr. Plant's guidance, and, although the *how* didn't much matter anymore, the *why* remained important. Jay was determined to fulfill his purpose, which he wholly believed was to heal. He was glad Kathy shared that ambition and even more so that they would pursue it side by side.

With only one year left in medical school and residency to follow, he reflected on those past opportunities he'd embraced on a whim and promised himself he would always say 'yes' when others would say 'no'.

3

Residency & A Change in the Plan

St. Raphael's Hospital for Children predominately cared for indigent families. This was, in part, due to its location in North Cincinnati, an area known for its high crime and low income. Jay didn't know it yet, but St. Raph's would teach him more about himself than it would about medicine, veering his course in a slightly different direction.

In the beginning, Jay absolutely loved pediatric internship and residency. He delighted in the feeling he got from working in a hospital that focused on treating families in need. He felt filled with mission and meaning as he learned and healed. It didn't take long for him and Kathy to fall into a steady, comfortable routine, balancing their medical training and personal lives. And, as much as he loved the reliable cadence he had with her, he quickly soured on that very aspect at the hospital.

"I just can't see myself being content with teaching parents how to introduce vegetables into their toddler's diet or assessing growth and intellectual progress by quizzing kids on colors and the sounds animals make. I feel like I wouldn't be able to make enough of a difference," Jay said to Kathy as he folded his scrubs and re-situated the items inside his modified gym bag. "You're lucky. You know exactly what you want to do, and it's well within your grasp. Me, I'm not so sure, but I do know it's not general pediatrics," he continued.

Kathy turned away from the Reds game they were only half-watching, half-listening to and redirected her attention to Jay. "Then change your concentration. We're only 6 months in, so it's simple enough. Just because you adored your pediatrician growing up doesn't mean you won't be adored unless you become that very thing. But Jay….it might mean a fellowship, woooooo," Kathy teased, making spooky motions with her hands.

"Oh, shut it!" Jay retorted and playfully tossed his scrub cap at her.

Dodging it, Kathy said, "Seriously though, Jay, have you thought about a specialty? Remember how much you loved helping in the pediatric intensive care unit (PICU) earlier this year? Why not pursue that?"

Jay continued to fold and think – think and fold – before responding, "Funny you should say that because that's actually what I am leaning towards. I *did* enjoy my time there, and I could definitely make a difference. The physiology is fascinating. It's not like you'd grow bored with inserting lines (IVs) or tubes (for ventilators). I'm not sure I could do the NICU (neonatal intensive care unit) though. Those babies are way too small! I'd be afraid of hurting them just by holding them!"

"…and that ball is outta here!" the voice of Johnny Bench boomed from the TV, signaling a Reds homerun.

Kathy clapped her hands together as she stood up to

return her ice cream bowl to the kitchen and declared, "Then it's settled. You'll move into the PICU rotation, and I'll do the same in Emergency Medicine. That way, at least *one* of us will have a more flexible schedule in case we ever want to have kids…and raise them ourselves!" Kathy tossed a pillow at Jay and walked into the kitchen. Jay finished preparing his bag for his rotation the next day, satisfied with everything in the path she'd just laid out.

***

Jay entered his PICU rotation expecting to rekindle the fire that general pediatrics had practically extinguished through its repetitive nature. He knew the four-week rotation would be grueling, and he was right. He readily adjusted to the different sleep pattern as well as to treating the kids with asthma, concussions, infections, even sickle cell anemia and cerebral palsy. These cases came and went successfully, and he enjoyed having a hand in their success stories. However, he quickly discovered that he may have traded in the flatness of general pediatrics for more than he could handle.

On the second Saturday of his rotation, Jay drove home in silence. He focused on the road ahead while the noise from the surrounding cars and such outside hummed around him. The sunset ahead was dull and lusterless, adding to the ominous feeling already looming. Lost in thought, Jay did not notice the annoying static whining intermittently from the radio.

Pulling into his parking space, he felt a surge of relief when he saw Kathy's car nestled in amongst the neighbors'. He had been hoping she'd be home when he arrived. He hardly made it into the apartment before breaking down about the events of his day. Kathy had seen it in his face the moment he crossed the threshold and rushed over to find out what had happened. He needed little encouragement to open up.

"...and if the worst is realized, I'll have to say those awful words out loud to his parents," Jay stopped and bowed his head in sorrow. Kathy wrapped her arms around him. She leaned her head into his neck and gently rocked him while he silently cried.

When he was able to, he continued. "Kathy, she looked me straight in the face with her tear-filled, reddened eyes and pleaded for reassurance, for a hope I couldn't give her. I just keep hearing her weeping and saying, 'It couldn't have been more than a minute! It couldn't have! And the kiddie pool was only a few feet deep! He'll be OK, won't he, Doctor? He'll be OK?' It keeps replaying and echoing in my head." He anguished at the thought and resumed crying.

"Honey, just like I said last night, you are doing everything you can for Billy. You guys were able to stabilize his physiology and bring back his heart and lungs! That's something! I know you're afraid of the EEG tomorrow, and if it doesn't find any brain activity, if the worst happens, I can think of no doctor I'd rather hear that news from. You truly care, Jay, and it shows. Even in times like these, *especially* in times like these, your humanity and kindness resonate." Kathy did her best to console him, but nothing seemed to work.

"Don't you get it?!" he screamed. "This isn't a physiology experiment! It's not a simulation or a reading assignment! It's a real-life, beautiful 4-year-old child! He's someone's little boy, and I can't save him!" He pulled free from Kathy's embrace, struggling with the overwhelming emotions. She went towards him, trying to get him to look at her, to focus on her words.

"Jay, now you listen to me!" She snapped her fingers in his face. "Of course, I know that this is a real little boy and not some experiment! But that doesn't change how you approach it. It may change how other physicians approach it, but I know you, and I know that you care regardless of whether it's real or hypothetical. You want to know how I know?? Because of this right here, your reaction. You want to heal. You're invested in each patient beyond their illness.

"You may not even notice this about yourself, but whenever we talk about how our days went, you always tell me about the kid who loves playing baseball in the backyard with his dad or the mom who can't wait to pick the flowers they planted together. You don't ever tell me about the boy whose lungs collapsed from cystic fibrosis or the girl who got a concussion from falling when using the fence as a balance beam. You see and care about more than the illness or injury, and that's what I love about you.

"You're going to be a great doctor, Jay. But you can't beat yourself up like this. You aren't going to be able to save them all, honey. I tell myself the same thing every time I go into the emergency room. If I didn't, I'd fall apart. If the worst happens, you will deliver the news in the most gentle way possible, better than anyone else could...*because* you care."

She stepped back, holding him by the arms straight out in front of her. He slowly raised his head to meet her gaze with his swollen, wet eyes. No more words were needed. Nothing could take away his sorrow over Billy's condition. Knowing that she not only supported him, but understood him so well, gave him sanctuary.

When he walked through the hospital doors the next morning to begin his rounds, he knew this day would change him. The tragedy of it all was so sudden and complete. Billy's heart and lungs remained stable, but his pupils didn't react to light, his body didn't flinch from pain, his reflexes couldn't be triggered. Billy's brain was dead. The only things keeping him alive were the life-support machines.

Billy's mother asked Jay a lot of questions, and slowly, he made her understand his level of helplessness and hopelessness. He never uttered the actual words, but she found her answers in his eyes. Two days later, Billy died in the arms of his grieving parents after being taken off life-support. Jay was with them, crying alongside. He went home that night and cried more to Kathy.

***

Jay viewed the rest of his time in PICU through a different lens after Billy. The children with terminal cancer and severe burns and deformities began to depress him. Before Billy, he viewed these cases as potential healing moments, positive stories birthed from dire situations. Now, the helplessness of the children, their parents and even the doctors overwhelmed him. He no longer went home and shared the events of his day with Kathy. He would listen to her talk about her day in the emergency room. The variety of cases she tended to was sure to keep any skilled medical professional on their toes, but the majority of them resulted in a positive or, at least hopeful, outcome, and they weren't all children.

Kathy noticed Jay's withdraw and wanted to give him

time to heal from, what he viewed as, a failure. A failure that resulted in the death of a child. But after weeks of gloominess, she knew she had to help coax him towards reconciling.

"Jay?"

"Hmm?" Jay replied robotically while staring through the television, as he seemed to do every night until he fell asleep now.

"You can't let this consume you any longer. I completely understand how traumatic and tragic losing a patient is, especially a child and in such a sudden manner. I do. But, honey, you're going to be a physician. You know that this is part of it. You have to move forward," she cautiously urged.

Jay didn't turn to look at her. He didn't seem to react to her words. He just sat there, gazing at the TV as if he would find absolution on the screen.

"Jay, are you hearing me? You're no good to anyone in this state. It's not healthy. You, of all people, know what depression can do to someone…to a family," she added, hoping the reference to his father's struggle, one he had ultimately lost, would jolt Jay out of this funk.

Turning to her with glassy eyes, he made a motion to speak but stopped before any sound escaped. Kathy remained curled up on the other side of their couch, waiting patiently for him to gather himself. She knew this would take a toll on him, but she wasn't sure how long she should allow him to fixate on it before nudging him.

He remained motionless. "I called them today…" Jay admitted in an almost inaudible tone. "I called them to see how they were holding up. They were thankful for my concern but asked me not to call again…" he paused once more, reliving the conversation in his head. His eyes filled, and he took a deep breath before going on. "My role in their lives is over, and I failed. I failed Billy, and I failed them." He was barely able to finish the last sentence before his grief took over and reduced him to sobs.

Kathy quickly moved to him, embracing him, and tried to repair the broken man in her arms. She whispered, "You did not fail anyone. You did everything you could do. No one could have produced a different outcome for that family. It wasn't because you did the wrong thing or didn't react in time or didn't know enough. Billy was gone when he was brought to you. This is not your failure. Accidents happen. Bad things happen. But so do good things.

"How many lives have you already helped in just the short time you've been a resident? Why aren't you running around, talking about all your successes? Hmm? You're not doing that because, as you would say, 'it's all part of the job.' Well, so is loss. The only thing you can do now is brush yourself off, apply the things you learned from it to future cases, and continue to work to heal." She squeezed him a little harder, hoping her words would not just be heard but felt as well.

Jay leaned into Kathy's embrace. He knew she was right. He also knew he couldn't do the PICU for a career. He didn't want to be sad like this again. He didn't want to cry every day. He wanted to stop reliving that moment, to stop staring at Billy's empty bed whenever he passed by.

"Thank you," he breathed into Kathy. He mustered a weak smile and nodded his head as if acknowledging that something internal was closing that chapter. "Thank you," he repeated.

***

Moving into his third and final year of residency, Jay, once again, redirected himself by deciding to dedicate his life and career to neonatology. He knew he wanted to work with children and since general pediatrics hadn't struck the chord, and the PICU situation left him depressed, the NICU was the next logical option. He figured he could roll the dice on hurting an infant simply by holding it.

The NICU field, itself, interested him, and he saw tremendous opportunity to be part of something bigger than himself. Its research was beginning to see success. Younger and younger preterm infants were being saved. Jay viewed neonatology as an opportunity to still evaluate and perform the procedures of a PICU doctor without having to treat the children suffering from burns or near drownings. It was a way he could still help without crying during, or after, every rotation.

Of all the intensive care units, adult and pediatric, the NICU had the best outcomes. Preterm babies were becoming little miracles. The field was advancing rapidly, and babies that started off so small, who could sometimes fit in the palm of your hand, were starting to make out of the unit. There was a happy excitement in the NICU around all the progress being made.

Of course, Jay still lost patients as some babies died, but it did not happen very often. He found it incredibly rewarding to see a very preterm infant grow under his care into a healthy baby ready for hospital discharge. Most importantly, the loss of a preterm baby was far less tragic, for both Jay and the family, than losing a child who was full of life one minute and gone the next.

Finally, the shoe fit, enabling him to continue down the path on his mission to heal, and he wore it to his fellowship across town at the Children's Hospital of Cincinnati (CHOC) every day.

4

Clinical Service & Separate Realities

The ring sat snuggly in its box inside his pocket where he'd placed it a few hours earlier. Despite his activity that day offering no chance for the box to leave that location, he found himself checking on it regularly. As they turned onto her parents' street, he was more concerned about her father's reaction than he was about getting a positive answer from Kathy.

"Honestly, Jay. It seems like every time we come here, you become a basket of nerves. When are you going to realize that no one cares that you're not Catholic! There are plenty of other reasons not to like you!" Kathy teased him in mild frustration as they parked the car.

"Oh, very funny. Ha. Ha," he mocked, once again checking on the ring's whereabouts.

"Well, you'd think after 5 years of dating, you would know they all like you by now."

They walked towards the house, carrying their luggage and multiple bags containing an assortment of Christmas presents and holiday-themed serving platters. They had come to spend the holidays with her family, as they had done each year since they'd gotten together.

"OK, deep breath, Nervous Nelly!" Kathy joked before opening the door and crossing the threshold into a wave of welcoming smells coming from the kitchen and the cozy fire burning in the living room fireplace.

Over the next few days, Jay looked for the most opportune time to ask Roger for his daughter's hand in marriage. He knew he had no reason to fear the man the way he did, but he couldn't help it. Maybe it was his dark eyes that seemed to communicate more than his mouth. Perhaps, it was the unwavering confidence he exuded at all times. Whatever it was, it made Jay incapable of feeling at ease in his presence. However, he *was* at ease with his decision to ask Kathy to marry him, and this was a critical step in going about that in the right way. So, on the last day of their visit, he was determined to find an opportunity.

Roger was in his usual spot on the couch, flipping through the TV channels when Jay nervously approached and sat down on the center cushion, awkwardly close to him. Roger looked him up and down out of the corner of his eye and asked, sarcastically, if everything was ok.

"Yes," replied Jay who stared at him in seriousness. "I have been waiting to get you alone this whole week, actually." He verified the ring's placement for a millionth time, closed his eyes and slowly drew in a deep breath. Roger recoiled as he watched Jay's hand slide across his pocket several times, unsure what to make of it in combination with Jay's closed eyes and heavy breathing.

"Mr. Nasci…" Jay began. "As you know, Kathy and I have been dating for about 5 years now, and I love her very much…I would like to ask you an important question." He paused, puzzled by the look on Roger's face, but decided to press ahead before the moment became even more awkward. "May I have permission to marry your daughter?" The question came out like a splinter, painful until the moment it was out. Already relieved, he waited for Roger's response.

Roger sat there, remote still in hand, for what felt like an eternity to Jay. Finally, he leaned forward, fixing his eyes on Jay's, clapped him on the back in a half-embrace and said, "Jesus, Jay! You had me scared for a minute! I thought you were gonna hit on me!"

"Wh..what??" Jay stuttered, unable to comprehend Roger's interpretation of the way that scene had played out.

"Yeah, you came in here, acting all weird, sitting so close. When you started rubbing your thigh with your eyes closed, I wasn't sure what the hell you had on your mind! I'm sure glad I was wrong!" Roger explained through laughter. "Of course, you have my permission to marry her! So long as you keep treating her the way you do now, we'll have no problems," he added in a more serious tone.

"I can assure you that I will not only take good care of your daughter, but that I also do not have those types of feelings for you," confirmed Jay, taking the ring from his pocket to show to Roger. "I'd like to ask her tonight, while we're still here, so she can share the moment with all of you."

"I think that'd be nice, son. Now, would you mind sliding over a bit? Regardless of your motive, you're crowding me," Roger requested with a smile. He selected a sports highlight show, and the two in-laws to-be watched together in silence, waiting for the women to return home from the store.

***

Jay's neonatology fellowship virtually flew by for him. His logic behind selecting that focus had been sound, fulfilling his mission and desire to heal without the intensity that accompanied the PICU rotations. During that time, Kathy slipped into her new job in the Emergency Department, quickly learning all of the tricks of the trade. She liked the shift-work mentality of the ED. She didn't have to bring her work home with her, and her hours were set, but she also found it very challenging and, sometimes a little scary. Being the only doctor in a busy emergency room can be a challenge and each day she would come home and tell Jay of another story.

Their future looked bright. Jay and Kathy bought a house, now that they were each on track towards their respective careers; Kathy continuing at Cincinnati Hospital and Jay set to return to St. Raphael's. It seemed the path had smoothed.

Not much had changed at St. Raph's since his residency other than his confidence. Jay returned with no more than the typical fear and excitement that accompanied anyone beginning a new position and jumped right into the NICU environment with the other attending physicians, many of whom had been his instructors a few short years ago. He was eager to learn the new systems and processes and prove himself to the group. However, that effort would pale in comparison to the task of convincing the nurses that he had honed his craft since his days as a resident.

As a whole, he loved being an attending physician (attending, for short). His fellowship had confirmed the career path he'd chosen, but he found himself surprised by how thoroughly he enjoyed every aspect of being on clinical service and taking care of the babies in the unit. Jay tried to approach this new phase of his career correctly. He recognized that being a good doctor involved more than medical knowledge and bedside manner, that cultivating healthy working relationships with the team was just as crucial to a physician's success. Any hospital-based doctor knew that nurses were not only the life energy of the hospital but key members of the team. A solid relationship with the nursing staff is advantageous in countless ways.

He'd shown up early for his shift, as he often did, to examine every baby and hear updates on any overnight issues from the bedside nurse. This extra time in the morning also allowed him to chat and become more acquainted with the team.

"All went well, so we were able to lower the ventilator settings throughout the night," Joan, a veteran nurse, informed Jay as he evaluated a preterm baby named Megan.

"That's wonderful." He made a note on her chart. "Let's plan to extubate today then. I can't imagine having a tube in your mouth is very comfortable," Jay replied while still reviewing the remaining data within. He was doing his best to assert himself as in control and not let on to the intimidation that still lingered from when he'd been working with Joan as a resident.

"If you want my two cents, Doctor, she's just started feeding well. It could stress her if we take her off the ventilator too soon. Of course, it's up to you, but that's my opinion," Joan stated, folding her arms across her chest.

Jay's ears were plugged with his stethoscope and his mind focused on listening to Megan's chest. "Yes, yes. Of course," he replied without breaking his concentration.

Had he looked up to respond, he would have seen Joan glaring her 20+ years of experience into the back of this

(what was *also* her opinion) arrogant, wet-behind-the-ears
attending. Instead, Jay finished his exam of baby Megan,
removed his stethoscope, made a few additional notes in
her chart, and moved on to the next patient. Joan unfolded
her arms in a silent huff and remained at Megan's bedside
to resume her duties.

At 0900 sharp, he, Joan, and the team of residents
began rounding, as per the daily ritual for the attending,
head nurse and medical students. They gathered at each
baby's bedside where a resident would present the case and
proposed next steps of care to the group. As the attending,
Jay was supposed to educate the team on the proper course
of treatment by citing the latest research articles, sharing
personal experiences and imparting lessons learned or best
practices. The goal was to give them the necessary tools
and knowledge to arrive at the correct determination on
their own, but ultimately, Jay had the final say.

The rounding technique has been used and celebrated
for centuries and is part of every teaching hospital's morning
ritual. Since St. Raph had a 30-bed NICU, this could take
several hours to complete. For it to be effective, Jay needed
to provide the right amount of knowledge and guidance
while also allowing the student to make some decisions…
by noon. Anything after that was considered "poor attending."

The group of 5, on the tail-end of their rounds, gathered
around Megan's bed to discuss her case. They reviewed her
chart and listened to Joan's account of Megan's progression,
and, after little deliberation, decided to remove her ventilator, which was unintentionally aligned with Jay's initial
conclusion. Jay, secretly pleased that the group had arrived
at the same determination, began mapping out the process.

"We will remove the ventilator and place a small plastic tube, known as a nasal cannula, into her nostrils that will provide oxygen. We will then monitor her breathing to ensure she doesn't experience any extended apnea, causing bradycardia." The group nodded confidently. "Does anyone know what that is commonly referred to as?" Jay asked the group.

A female resident raised her hand. "Apnea, a temporary cessation of breathing, and bradycardia, an abnormally slow heart action, are known as As and Bs."

"That is correct, almost exactly so," confirmed Jay. "A preterm baby takes approximately 40 breaths per minute compared to the 12 an average adult takes." Teaching was his favorite part. "If an apnea pause lasts longer than 20 seconds, bradycardia, or the slowing of the heartrate, occurs." He paused to assess the attention of the group, which remained intact. "While As and Bs are very common in preterm babies, if their frequency increases, it's always best to have the attending evaluate and rule out any other contributing factors or developing issues."

Jay paused once again, this time to answer several questions before resuming. "Does anyone know the proper protocol should the As and Bs become concerning?"

The same resident raised her hand. "First, we stimulate the baby with a gentle touch in an effort to wake them to breathe. If that doesn't discontinue or decrease the frequency or potency of the apnea, we would order caffeine. If there is still no improvement, the baby is placed on a ventilator."

"Correct again," verified Jay. "And since you've answered both questions for us in this scenario, we'll have you administer the nasal cannula."

The group shuffled about, preparing for the procedure while Jay updated his rounding notes. Once again, Jay failed to see the daggers Joan's eyes aimed at him. Despite the group's justification, she still disagreed with removing Megan from the ventilator so soon and stood there watching in disapproval as they carried out their course of treatment, wishing Jay would have prompted a more collaborative discussion of care that involved her input in addition to her account.

After monitoring Megan off the ventilator for some time, the team, satisfied with her stability, moved on to baby Michael, their final bedside. Joan reluctantly followed.

With no action to take after reviewing baby Michael's progress, the group dispersed to resume their regular operational tasks. Joan, released from the responsibility of rounding, circled back to Megan to check on her condition.

She watched the baby's impossibly small chest rise and fall with short, shallow breaths that were intermittently interrupted by brief pauses. Although she knew this was still within the boundaries of normal, something kept her unsettled. She shifted her weight to her other foot and positioned her wristwatch out in front, in line with the view of Megan's breathing, and began timing the apnea intervals. About 25 minutes later, she called Jay over.

"The frequency is too often for my liking, Dr. Greenspan," Joan informed.

"OK. How long is each pause on average?" inquired Jay, interpreting Joan's concern as an attempt to undermine his decision to remove the ventilator or, at best, an overreaction.

"Not very long, 10 to 15 seconds on average, and though she is responding to stimulation, they keep happening, and it's not sitting right with me," declared Joan, who didn't miss the young attending's apathetic tone.

Jay gently placed his stethoscope onto Megan's tiny chest and listened once again before instructing Joan to continue tracking the pauses and durations and call him if they went outside of the parameters he then set forth. Jay was confident that Megan would be fine once she adjusted to being off the ventilator and even more confident that Joan was simply using this to make a point.

The two of them bounced around the ward, like an advanced level in Pong. Joan, monitoring the apnea, moved with purpose back and forth between Megan and the other babies' bedsides. Jay, busy with the duties of an attending, incorporated additional observations of her into his regular routine as allowed. However, after a few hours and multiple escalated interventions, it became clear that nothing was working to stop the little patient's apnea. It was time to place her back on the ventilator.

Jay called the team of residents back to Megan then he and Joan worked together synchronously to get her more stable. And while the "I told you so" hovered in the air between them, Joan didn't say anything outside of the necessary communication throughout the process, carrying out her responsibilities reflexively alongside the green attending.

Once things had calmed down and Megan had re-established an even breathing pattern, Jay flew his charred yet salvageable chariot down and thanked Joan for her assistance. Pleased with the overall outcomes – a stabilized patient and humbled doctor – she graciously nodded.

When it came to the health of children, pride and egos had to be sidelined. Some learned to both offer *and* accept guidance while others refused to acknowledge their inexperience. The important difference in the two types was how they handled the aftermath. In Joan's long career, she'd encountered enough supercilious doctors to know when to supplement an error in judgement with a lecture and when the near-miss, itself, is sufficient for that purpose.

No one, except perhaps Joan, had any way to know that Megan would successfully extubate several days later and move on to be just fine. Another fact, also privy only to Joan, was that her and Jay's working relationship would not heal as quickly. However, his unspoken acknowledgement of his initial pretention was the first step in the treatment.

***

"Well, I have no way of knowing whether or not the extubation failure was inevitable. They're too unpredict-able," Jay justified over dinner with Kathy that following weekend. "I mean, all that matters is that she ended up successfully extubating in the end, but I know Joan's revel-ing in the fact that she was right. She's always been a tough nut to crack." Jay shook his head, dismissively, as he swirled his pasta around his fork and took a sip of his wine.

"Tough or not, you need to repair the disconnect between the two of you. Good nurses have a 'sixth sense' and sometimes know the babies better than any doctor can since they spend so much time bedside. It would behoove you to always respect and leverage the individual perspec-tive of your teammates, and in this case, Joan," Kathy replied before taking a bite of her own pasta dish.

"I highly doubt *that* would have changed anything other than the number of trips back and forth I made to her bed," Jay snorted but quickly changed his tone when he saw the disapproving look on Kathy's face.

"Regardless of whether she truly had cause for concern or was capitalizing on the situation to knock you down a few pegs, the fact remains that you're the 'newb' in the unit she's been working in for over 20 years. How would you like it if some new doctor waltzed in, thinking they knew more than you?" No response came from Jay's side of the table.

"Exactly," she said, punctuating the air with her fork. "So, ask her for advice on the patients she spends so much time with and then heed it. Show that you value her experience and welcome her mentorship. Worst case, you make no headway with her and she remains cold. Best case, you learn a few things, have the support of the head nurse, and maybe make a new friend, right? You've gotta look to and use the perspectives of everyone on the team, Jay. You all may work in the same environment, but it won't always look the same to everyone. Use that. It can only benefit you and, more importantly, the patient."

Jay considered Kathy's words while he ate a big bite of linguini. He grinned at her and said, "How did you get to be so smart, and how did I get to be so lucky?"

She blushed and raised her glass to his with a smirk. "Don't talk with your mouthful, Jay. Honestly, I don't think I have time to teach you anything else before dessert comes," she laughed and playfully rolled her eyes.

5

Researching & Volunteering
Discretionary Effort

When not on clinical service, an academic neonatologist was required to teach and get involved in research. Jay hadn't had any desire to pursue the latter since being an undergrad, and even then, it had only barely caught his attention. The former, however, came naturally, and he greatly enjoyed passing on his knowledge to any attentive residents wanting to learn.

Jay often found himself giving impromptu talks on a variety of neonatal topics throughout the day. The residents seemingly appreciated his willingness to mentor and capitalized on it by taking every available opportunity to run scenarios by him or asking him their unsolved questions. This became a regular part of Jay's hospital life, like a mother duck showing her ducklings the ropes.

Research didn't come as easy. During his fellowship, he'd had plenty of positive experiences and written a few papers, even presenting several at national meetings, yet failed to attain the enthusiasm and competence he'd practically assumed would emerge. He much preferred working with babies, continuing to learn the ropes of clinical care, and interacting with students. A year into his career as an attending and that hadn't changed. Good thing he hadn't become a botany researcher!

However, he knew he couldn't be promoted without research, so he had to dive into this aspect with an equal amount of passion and focus if he were to become the doctor and rising academic he anticipated. So, he stood over the preterm lamb lying on the table in the center of the small laboratory, awaiting instruction.

"You'll notice that this 22-week-old's lungs have not yet generated enough surfactant to allow them to function without assistance, such as a ventilator. A main challenge for many preterm infants is lung disease, which directly results from the lack of surfactant, a natural soap if you will, that covers the surface of the lungs, keeping them slippery and open, preventing them from sticking together and eventually collapsing.

"From an evolutionary standpoint, this natural soap allowed mammals to leave the oceans and breathe air. The goal of our research is to use this concept to discover a way to allow humans to breathe a liquid again, which, we believe, may solve the problem of surfactant deficiency and reduce or even eliminate the need for respiratory assistance," finished Tom, the young yet very successful physiologist who ran this St. Raphael's associated laboratory.

Jay may not have enjoyed research as much as clinical service, but the concept of liquid ventilation intrigued him. After studying lung function in preterm babies during his fellowship, he'd opted to further explore neonatal lung physiology for this portion of his career. Plus, he'd worked with both Tom and his partner, Marla, a bit during his fellowship and, at a minimum, figured he would at least enjoy having them as mentors.

"Many liquids do not carry enough oxygen to enable breathing, as I'm sure you're all aware," Marla added, picking up where Tom left off. "However, through our research, we've found a special liquid, called perfluorocarbon, that does carry oxygen and is breathable." Her face beamed as she informed the group of this success of theirs.

"As pharmaceutical companies continue making artificial surfactants, we will continue to test our liquid ventilation against them. If the results remain consistent, we expect to keep finding that perfluorocarbons are better." Marla finished speaking and looked to Tom who displayed an equal amount of pride in his face.

The physiology made sense to Jay, and the successful supporting studies with preterm lambs boosted the appeal of it all. Over time, it became clearer and clearer to Jay that he was at the forefront of a new and very special treatment. He began spending a lot of time in the lab with Tom and Marla, talking about science and, eventually, lighter topics as well. He stayed after hours to clean up or run errands for them in hopes of earning their trust and, maybe, more responsibility.

The three of them began writing papers and presenting their research at meetings together. Kathy often joined them on these trips, shoring up their little laboratory family. It soon became routine for other neonatologists to approach them after a presentation to discuss the possibility of clinical trials. For Jay, only a year into the research, this was exciting. For Tom and Marla, who had devoted years to this, it was a long-awaited opportunity.

Jay knocked lightly on the door to the office Tom and Marla shared. Behind stacks of books and papers, two heads looked up from their individual work as they waved him in.

"First, I want to thank you both for granting me the privilege of working alongside you for the past two years. I have thoroughly enjoyed myself and all of the knowledge I've gained," Jay began.

Tom and Marla exchanged a concerned look, cringing as Jay continued, "Now that I have another year of lamb trials, honing my technique and presenting at scientific conferences under my belt, I feel I'm ready to take the next step." He paused to take a mental deep breath then proceeded. "This may be a bit premature – I *am* a neonatologist after all – but I would be honored if you would consider allowing me to lead a clinical trial in preterm infants." Jay stood there, expecting to be let down gently, when Tom and Marla erupted with laughter. Jay was hit with a shot of adrenaline as he became hot with embarrassment. He'd considered them having several different reactions to his proposal, but none of them included laughter. *Shit.*

"Oh man, Jay! You had us thinking you were going to leave us! So formal all of a sudden," they teased and exchanged another look to confirm the other's thoughts before Tom disclosed their silent agreement. "Jay, we would be honored to give you that responsibility! We've been waiting for someone to ask, in fact, and hoped it would be you!"

Jay remained standing there, unsure whether to trust his own ears. *Did they really just agree to me running the very first trial in liquid ventilation?!* he thought to himself. *And why does everyone initially misinterpret my intentions as something very different than their reality? Am I really that awkward?*

"Jay? Everything ok?" Marla nudged, waiting for the disbelief to release him.

"Yes, yes. I'm definitely ok! I'm just trying to wrap my head around what I just signed up for, where to begin, what I need to do next..." He trailed off, returning inside his brain to begin organizing the process. "Kathy isn't going to believe this!"

"Well, before you are off and running, why don't you call Kathy and invite her to a celebratory dinner for the four of us tonight? We all have an equal amount to celebrate!" Tom suggested, standing up to walk over and shake Jay's hand. "You pick the place!"

"OK! How does Italian sound?"

"Italian sounds wonderful," agreed Marla smiling with both pride and excitement. "Let's say 7:30. That gives us time to clean up the lab...and ourselves." She winked then returned her focus to the work on her desk.

***

Jay followed Kathy around the kitchen, like a shadow, while she emptied the dishwasher. He had so many tasks on his mental to-do list that he found it near impossible to do anything other than pace around, as if herding his thoughts.

"Well, assuming I'm able to get past all the regulatory research review boards, which comes *after* the elaborate process of even bringing liquid ventilation to the clinic, the infant selection has to be pristine," he informed her, using his fingers to bullet point the list while still tracking her footsteps.

"I mean, the ethics will be dicey no matter which way you look at it. The infants will have to be very sick and near death to try something this new. Obtaining true consent from the parents will be a science in and of itself! I'll have to be immensely careful not to raise their hopes too high, to kindly but clearly communicate that this is a last-ditch effort. And then, of course, there's—" Jay, quicky running out of fingers, was interrupted by Kathy who he'd somewhat forgotten was in the room as he talked through his thoughts aloud.

"Timeout! Slow down for a moment. This isn't the first time you've plunged into something without mapping out the full course first. Relax!" she encouraged. Jay narrowed his pacing radius and refocused his attention onto her.

"Think about it, Jay. You wouldn't even be having this discussion with me if you hadn't said 'yes' all those years ago at Connecticut College, right? I'd say that worked out pretty well for you, and you were *way* less prepared for that decision than you are right now," she pointed out.

Jay considered this for a moment. He was definitely no stranger to agreeing to or volunteering for things that may be slightly out of his reach. And he also wasn't a stranger to success, which is what he'd turned those situations into.

"I can be excited about this because I know what needs to be done, and I know how to achieve it. Albeit, the task isn't small, and neither is the risk, but this is what I got into medicine for in the first place; to heal," he voiced his epiphany out loud. Noticing Kathy looking at him oddly, he realized that he probably looked like a madman after pacing the kitchen, toggling between counting on his fingers and running them through his hair. And now, he was talking to himself. Out loud!

In a clumsy attempt to suddenly appear casual, he leaned against the counter and smoothed his hair, smiling at her. Although it was more awkward than convincing, this pause was exactly what he needed to gather himself and calm down. He could be excited, but there was no reason for the train to derail. He trusted his partners. He had confidence in himself. He knew the whole process – the thoughts, plans, tasks, boxes to check, equipment to setup, all of it – would be organized, followed, and completed.

Once again, Kathy managed to grab his string and pull him back down to the ground, this time without much effort. Acknowledging this, he was able to stifle the chaos of ideas and undertakings in his brain and be present with her for the rest of the evening. He wasn't, however, able to stifle his anticipation.

6

Clinical Trials & Being Humanistic

Death was just moments away. Tom, Marla, and Jay raced to assemble their rudimentary equipment designed for a quick set up. Although it was far less sophisticated than what they used in the laboratory, they were hopeful it would work all the same. After all, they'd thoroughly tested it and, outside of being bulky, it produced results, which this tiny infant desperately needed.

After being on the maximum ventilation possible, the baby girl was still not getting enough oxygen. Days of trying various things to help her did little to change her fate. As her heart rate stopped fluctuating and began drifting steadily downward, the NICU team prepared her parents for the worst, keeping their optimism low. With only one more option left, Jay obtained consent from the parents who had already begun grieving.

The room was bright and chilled. The smell of baby lotions, menthol and soap floated in the air, and the sounds from all the equipment pulsed, like timers on a gameshow, except there would be no consolation prize. Jay worried to himself about the possibility of success. All the liquid ventilation studies they'd done to date had been performed on lambs right after birth, not days later on a human, which made him wonder if this infant's preterm lung disease would respond to the new therapy. In the absence of any alternative solutions, they began the process.

The team, wide-eyed and hopeful, watched the liquid travel through her tube and into her body and, almost instantly, trigger a bradycardia episode. They exchanged quick, pensive looks in unspoken collaboration, deciding whether to continue the procedure. However, before reaching a decision, her teeny heart regained control and the rate picked back up, striving to reach normal. A collective sigh was released as they continued observing her response to their treatment. The resolved bradycardia episode was just a small victory, the battle had not yet been won. They needed her blood oxygen saturation to increase as well.

The liquid dripped into her lungs, moving in and out at a slow 5 breaths per minute. Her parents, along with the group of doctors and nurses, were full of trepidation, breathing at a similar pace. They watched her vital signs closely while studying her lung function. Although she displayed hints of improvement, there was minimal change in either her heart rate or blood saturation.

Come on, little one, thought Jay. *Come on...*

The room felt smaller and darker. The silence was so apparent that it taunted them, growing the shared and already intense apprehension. Several more excruciating minutes passed when an encouraging beep snatched their attention. Her oxygen levels had begun to climb. Before this was able to be processed and any of their hopes could follow suit, her heart rate unexplainedly and abruptly dropped.

There was no time to troubleshoot or see if it would stabilize. They had to immediately abort the procedure and return her to gas ventilation, which stopped her heart's nosedive but promised nothing else. A faint whimper escaped the mother's mouth and was met by her husband's consoling shush. Disconnecting their equipment created a brief rustle of footsteps and activity around the baby. Afterward, no one said anything. They all just stood there, silently willing the girl to live.

She died thirty minutes later.

Once her parents had gone and the reality began to set in, Tom, Marla and Jay stood at her bedside saddened by the results, or lack thereof, of their technique. Packing up their equipment, the trio posed questions aloud without the expectation of answers. *Had they made a mistake in the technique? Was the protocol flawed? Would this therapy that seemed so magical in preterm lambs work on humans? Had they simply been too late to help?*

Back in the lab, the team regrouped and reviewed the data they had collected. Despite Tom pointing out several positive, useful findings, little could console Jay who felt overwhelmed by all the unknowns. He had been so hopeful only to watch another life slip away.

***

Over the next 6 weeks, Tom, Marla, and Jay tried their procedure on two other infants in very similar situations to the first little girl. The results were also similar with small measures of success, but not enough to maintain life. The group decided to halt the trial and reevaluate the data and approach.

Shifting their focus from trials to additional analysis,

they expanded certain elements and validated their refined theories. They were invited to present their initial experience in a platform presentation at a national meeting in Washington DC a few months later. Tom suggested that Jay be the presenter, since he was the clinician.

With the 10-minute presentation prepared and practiced countless times, they traveled to the convention where they joined the sea of neonatologists absorbing the lectures focused on fine-tuning the techniques that were proving so successful in the NICU. Every doctor wanted to be on the cutting edge of this new field. Jay sat in his seat, fidgeting while he went over his talk in his mind, the voices of the other presenters echoing in distortion as he scrutinized every nuance of his upcoming address.

He was brought back to the large, theater-style auditorium by Tom's clammy handshake and Marla's well-wishing. It was his turn. He side-stepped out of his row and walked down the aisle, willing his legs to support him as he climbed the steps to the stage. He gripped the podium and realized that it was his hands that were clammy, not Tom's. *Calm down, Jay,* he urged himself.

His slides were projected on 3 large screens that spanned the width of the room, illuminating the audience. Jay looked out on the standing-room-only crowd of attentive faces and felt his legs weaken. *You got this. You know it backwards and forwards. Relax!* Taking a deep breath in, Jay delivered his talk on pure adrenaline and muscle memory. And, after an impossibly long 15 minutes passed, Jay heard the moderator thank him and open the floor to questions. He stood in place at the podium, willing his breathing to regulate and heart rate to quiet down as a long line formed at the audience microphone.

Doctor after doctor waited for a turn to address the young, quaking neonatologist. Jay saw rows of white-haired and balding men who looked like they had been running NICUs since he was smoking in the arboretum as an undergrad and wished he were back there. Tom and Marla listened to him field each comment, willing him strength to endure the forum. Part of them was happy not to be up there while the other part knew that this was how all novel therapies had to start and that Jay would handle it and grow from the experience.

The presentation was scrutinized. Their research efforts were criticized and physiological assumptions critiqued. But worst and most upsetting, their ethics were questioned.

"How can you *truly* obtain informed consent from the parent of a dying baby?" a fellow physician demanded.

Jay had prepared for this question, if only when asking himself the very same thing during each trial.

"We did our best. We took the data we had and tried to make the right decisions." He looked straight out at the audience, knowing that the only thing he could offer was the truth and hope that, as fellow physicians, they would be able to relate.

He struggled through the 10-minute session only to be saved by the bell, like a boxer fighting to remain upright until the end of the round. He thanked everyone for their time then descended the stage and returned to his seat by Tom and Marla.

"You did great, Jay," Marla reassured.

Tom nodded and added, "This will be one of those memories we will laugh about 20 years from now."

Jay was still too shell-shocked to relax, the comments reeling in his brain, causing doubt and disappointment. If it had worked, they would have been heroes. But it had not, and three lives were unable to be saved.

Tom and Marla calmly managed the inquiries that trickled in as the conference adjourned, and they all made their way towards the exits, giving Jay time to collect his thoughts and process their research's reception. The shuffling and murmurs of the attendees dispersing and discussing the new information relayed in the presentations dominated the room. Thus, Jay did not notice the seasoned neonatal researcher approaching until he had been greeted.

"Dr. Greenspan?" A hand extended towards him. "Dr. Turco, Boston Children's. I wanted to compliment you on an authentic and humanistic presentation."

Jay paused before accepting the man's hand and shaking it. "Thank you. I appreciate your kind words," he replied still skeptical from the forum's negative feedback.

"Don't let the others get to you." Dr. Turco swatted casually towards the auditorium. "There will always be critics, especially of those who try to advance the field of medicine. It's unproductive behavior, to criticize. However, the same could be said for allowing it to affect your work. All you can do is your best and be humble in defeat, which is what I saw in the three of you up on that stage."

"Yes, well, we certainly try…" Jay shrugged, caught off-guard by the praise.

"That's all you can do," he repeated. "I've been in your shoes and know the feeling. I admire your efforts and the courage of your team. Keep up the good work. There are infants still dying that need doctors like you. Don't let a little criticism derail things. It's better to be criticized than to have nothing *to* criticize." He smiled in an almost fatherly way and shook Jay's hand once more before excusing himself and making his way towards the door.

Jay was surprised by the impact Dr. Turco's words had on him. He had needed a quick pick-me-up with a side of kick-in-the-pants to remember to get back up and carry on. Suddenly, he heard his father's voice remind him that he could only control his own actions. A mix of somber and calming emotions surfaced, and Jay allowed himself to wade into the memories of those heart-to-hearts he so dearly missed.

It's not you, Jay, he'd said. *It's everyone else. They're the ones with the problem. Move on, and don't let them get you down. And when you're up, be sure to think with the head on your shoulders.* Jay smiled and let out a relieved chuckle. His father had always had a way of making light of a situation while also providing valuable insight. *I guess even death can't stop him from making a Freudian joke,* Jay thought.

Feeling his optimism reviving, he took his late father's advice, brushed himself off and focused on the doctor from Boston's praise, vowing to always remain genuine in motive and human in approach. After all, doing so had gotten him this far.

***

Jay entered his fourth year since graduating from his fellowship and, when not on service, continued his research with Tom and Marla, tediously examining the data from their failed trials, refining their techniques, and exploring other viable resources to better the treatment process, which resulted in additional discoveries unrelated to liquid ventilation as well.

They began publishing a great deal of their research,

which strengthened their cause and credence and eventually led to a call from a company in California that was interested in doing a larger, multi-institution trial of preterm infants with lung disease. Having read the studies, they wanted to try the treatment, this time enrolling infants closer to birth rather than waiting until after the ventilator did irreparable damage, which normally occurred after just one week of life. The trio felt ready to try again and was thrilled by the opportunity.

The news of this bolstered Jay's ascent on the academic ladder just as the time for promotion to associate neared. It was understood that, after beginning as an instructor, the next rung in the ladder was assistant followed by associate, ending as full professor. Jay had been very careful to meet each item on the long list of promotion requirements in anticipation of the next step in his career.

While he sat at his desk preparing his application, the phone rang. Initially, Jay ignored the ringing, knowing it wasn't an emergency, since those came through on his pager first, but finally decided to answer just in case.

"Jay?" said a vaguely familiar voice from inside the receiver.

"Yes?" Jay couldn't quite place it.

"Hey there! It's Patrick Seybert. How are you?"

Patrick! That's who it was! Jay instantly recognized the voice belonging to his mentor from his fellowship program. "Patrick! I'm well! I'm well! How are things with you? To what do I owe this pleasure?"

"Good, good. No complaints over here. I'm at Sherman now, leading a division of their neonatology department. I'm actually calling because I'd like to bring you on board my team..." Patrick trailed off, waiting for Jay's reaction.

Jay had always assumed he would see Patrick again at the next conference or summit, maybe somewhere random in the city. And while he considered Patrick a good mentor and colleague, he certainly hadn't expected Patrick to call him for any reason, much less to offer him a job. However, he didn't dwell on the surprise of either occurrence. Instead, he focused on the proposal.

Sherman was part of an esteemed medical school, but it wasn't a children's hospital, such as St. Raph's. This did not imply inferiority, rather it simply meant that its NICU was likely much smaller and less equipped. Since babies are not delivered at children's hospitals, many of those with delivery services, like Sherman, will have a small NICU but ultimately transfer any cases they cannot manage to children's hospitals where they have specialists and more specialized equipment.

"Wow, Patrick. I'm flattered…but I'm not really looking to make a move at the moment," Jay admitted. "I'm sorry—"

"Hear me out." Patrick interrupted Jay, ready with his pitch. "I know what you're thinking. Why move from a children's hospital when you're a neonatologist, right?"

"Well…" Jay rubbed the back of his neck, determining how to let his former mentor down easy. "It doesn't make much sense, does it?" he asked in earnest as he finished contemplating the idea.

"I guess that depends on what your individual goals are. Are we a children's hospital? No, but we are a teaching one and, because of that, we have better equipment and a few surgeons and specialists staffed in our NICU."

"Your nursery *is* pretty large, considering—" Jay started.

"Yes! And we are doing some great research!" Patrick

exclaimed. "Listen, Jay. I am prepared to make you an offer you can't refuse. I will double your salary, start you as associate director of the NICU, *and* guarantee your promotion to associate professor within a year." Jay could practically see the smile of satisfaction on Patrick's sharp-featured face.

"Wow. That *is* definitely an offer that's hard to refuse," Jay conceded. "But Patrick, it's not necessarily all about the money for me. See, I'm comfortable here at St. Raph's. I'm thriving in and enjoying my responsibilities. That's not to say I'm not honored that you thought of me—"

Patrick cut him short once again. "There's no need for you to answer me this minute. Take some time to think it over, discuss it with…Kathy, was it?"

Jay cleared his throat. "Uh, yes, Kathy is my wife's name."

"You married her! Wonderful!"

"Yes, thank you," Jay agreed, stumbling on Patrick's impressive recall. "Ok, Patrick. You've made a good case. I will consider your offer. I'll take your advice and, if it's ok with you, get back to you with my answer shortly."

"Perfect! I will look forward to your call, then. Thank you for hearing me out," Patrick said sincerely.

"No problem. Thank you for giving me the opportunity," replied Jay, equally as sincere.

The two exchanged full contact information before ending the call. *Double my salary? Associate director of the NICU? Guaranteed promotion?* Jay thought to himself.

"He wasn't kidding when he said, 'an offer I can't refuse'," Jay said out loud, snorting in disbelief. "Wait 'til Kathy hears *this* one!" Intrigued, he resumed filling out his application for promotion at St. Raph's with less intent than before.

***

"So, just like that, he offered to double your salary and make you associate director of the NICU?! Does he have that kind of authority?" Kathy asked in surprised disbelief after hearing the news.

"He must because he did. I've heard through the grapevine that Patrick 'wants in' on the next round of liquid ventilation trials. If they're successful, it could really boost Sherman's reputation. Plus, we all know that Patrick is an aggressive builder, whether it's a team or department, he doesn't stop until it's as strong as he can get it," Jay returned, reminding her of several instances during his fellowship.

"True, true. I forgot what a bulldog he could be. Well, this is an amazing opportunity. So, what are you thinking? Do you want to accept the offer?" Kathy probed, silently hoping Jay was leaning towards a decision either way so she didn't have to help him choose between the two. Both were good options with an almost equal amount of positive and negative elements. Deciding would be tough.

"Well, I owe it to Charlie to discuss it with him first. He's been a great boss, and I'm very happy at St. Raph's. I'd like to get his input and feel he will be straight with me. It's not like I was *looking* to leave, ya know?"

The couple carried on with their conversation, pointing out the benefits to each position, while painting the living room a color that better suited them. The muted shade of yellow the previous owners had selected didn't offer much to the ambiance. Perhaps, if they had gone with a more golden version, it could have had a warming effect, but they'd missed the mark and, instead, created a room that had the color and appeal of tobacco-stained teeth. Thus, new paint had been at the top of Kathy and Jay's project list upon move in. At the end of the evening, they were left with a soft, robin's egg blue room and a career move that hinged on Charlie's reaction to the offer itself.

7

A Small Ask & Courageous Conversation

The next day went by at an awkward pace. The meeting had been set for later that afternoon, giving Jay more time to further muddy the decision-making waters. For every good reason to leave, there was a good reason to stay. For instance, salary and title aside, the research opportunity associated with Patrick's offer was compelling. It would practically guarantee Jay more time, funding and support for his pursuits. Still, Jay had grown comfortable in his current work routine. The team worked well together, and Charlie, with his hands-off yet available management style, encouraged growth and development. So, when the time finally came to sit down with Charlie, Jay wasn't sure what he hoped would come from it.

"That's disappointing," Charlie guilted with raised eyebrows, his face otherwise devoid of emotion.

"I wasn't looking for this, if that's any consolation," Jay urged, hating the possibility of disappointing him.

"Ahh, but you're considering it," Charlie retorted, leaning forward and crossing his arms on his neatly organized desk. "So, what is my role in this decision you're to make? How can I help?"

Jay scratched the back of his head and readjusted his position in the chair. "Well, I guess I don't really know. I just felt it was best to tell you about the offer before I'd even made any decision."

"I see." Leaning back now, Charlie's gaze seemed to search Jay for an idea on which direction he intended to go. Finding none, he shifted his focus to the items slightly above and behind Jay where, perhaps, the answers might be. "I'll be honest with you. We would be sad to see you go. What would it take for you to stay?" he asked, now looking back at Jay.

"See, that's the thing. I'm not sure what there is to offer. The leadership of our unit is pretty well set, so there's not much room for upward mobility," Jay pointed out, half to Charlie and half to himself. He then reflected on the proximity of Sherman to the lab, which meant his research wouldn't be interrupted because the move would only take him across town. Without the academic risk, it basically boiled down to whether Jay wanted to leave the staff he'd grown comfortable with and fond of for more money and a promotion. But he couldn't say that, of course.

"Look, I'll be honest with you, too. I'm happy here. I really wasn't looking for anything else. If you could give me a small raise even, I could rest knowing I didn't decline an offer to double my salary without getting some sort of boost," Jay lobbied, thinking that he *should* expect *some* sort counteroffer simply as part of the dance. He knew Kathy would certainly expect him to get one!

"I wish I could, but I can't. The best I can do is recommend one, which I'm happy to do, but it's up to the department chairman." His face took on a slightly cynical expression, indicating the minimal value he saw in that pursuit. "We like having you here, you're a good leader and well-respected. Be sure to let me know if there is anything I *can* do to prevent you from leaving." Charlie stood and extended his hand to Jay. "You do what's best for you. It's what we all have to do."

"Thank you, sir," Jay said, shaking Charlie's hand. "I wish this were an easier decision to make."

"You'll figure out the right thing to do. You always seem to."

This kindness and encouragement from Charlie only made it harder for Jay to make a choice. Coming up empty-handed in that meeting only meant he had to make an appointment with the chairman and go through the whole negotiation process to ensure confidence in whichever position he chose. *Great,* he thought sarcastically as he sent an email to the chairman's assistant, scheduling the next step, which had him knocking on the office door of Dr. Dan Stephank a week later.

"Come in!" barked the normally quiet cardiologist who made very few appearances around the hospital floors.

I hope Charlie gave him a heads up about why I wanted to meet with him, thought Jay as he silently shut the door and entered the spacious office decorated with sharp-edged furniture the color of slate. He turned to face the chairman, whom he'd seen only a handful of times, never spoken to. As he mustered up his simple ask, he noticed how clean everything in the office looked, Dan included. Everything seemed to have a sheen.

"Well? What can I do for you?" Dan snapped impatiently. He signed a document then tossed the pen across the desk before taking his glasses off to clean them.

"I won't take up much of your time. I wanted to express my appreciation for all that St. Raphael's has done for me. The training and past four years of growth as a junior attending have been wonderful. I couldn't have asked for a better start to my career," Jay began.

"Start, huh? Ok, so is there an end? Get to your point, please."

Taken aback and unprepared to continue after being derailed by the chairman's abruptness, Jay fumbled briefly before finding his words.

"I received an offer from an old mentor of mine from my fellowship," Jay started to explain, filling him in on the details. "I'd need a small bump in salary to justify staying here," he stated, cringing internally. Jay hated negotiating. Actually, that wasn't entirely true. He had no issue advocating on behalf of someone else, it was negotiating for himself that he hated. It was this very reason why he'd not received a raise in over 4 years.

"What are you thinking?" spat Dan, grinning as if this was some sort of prank.

Jay froze. "I—I—"

"Are you seriously considering leaving a children's hospital for a lesser NICU where you will have no option for growth, no future??" He chuckled. "Money is nice, but it's not worth the death of an otherwise promising career. You need to be very careful about making a move like this. If you move to Sherman, you will never amount to anything."

Still frozen, Jay sat in the shiny room in the shiny chair, staring at the shiny man. *What a prick!* he thought. *Who does this guy think he is?*

"Thank you for the advice, sir. However, I *have* given

this serious thought. Unfortunately, I don't feel it's that black and white," he replied, sincerely. The two men sat silently across from one another until Dan asked if he needed to talk to him about anything else. Satisfied to hear that Jay was only there to discuss a small pay increase, he promptly declined the request and dismissed Jay from the office, closing the door behind him with a lusterless smile.

Thank you for making the decision for me. Jay shook his head at the outcome of the meeting and headed back to his comfortable office. He was left with no choice. The reasons to stay were not strong enough to warrant doing so, especially considering he received no additional compensation throughout the ordeal. However, as unpleasant as it had been, at least he'd tried. So, he notified Charlie that he would be leaving but waited two more days before calling Patrick to accept the position on the off chance that a raise came through. No such counteroffer ever did. And, after extinguishing the disapproval from his team by explaining his reasoning, all that was left to do was pack up his things, head across town, and start all over again.

8

A Fresh Start & Lessons Learned

Jay's tendency to say 'yes' when many would say 'no' (or at least 'hold on') was compounded by his training as an intensive care doctor. Rarely was he afforded time to weigh options when doing so could mean the difference between the life and death of a child. As a result, he'd become accustomed to timely decision making. His youthful inclination to knee-jerk react had been replaced with a rapid yet careful assessment of information.

Still, his capacity to determine the best option available then execute without second-guessing remained unchanged. His nature, reinforced by his medical nurture, gave Jay the ability to go 'all in' without hesitation. Maturity, responsibility, and experience added self-reflection and situational critique to his repertoire. These attributes were all coming together to create the beginnings of a competent, informed physician with a commitment to continuous improvement. Yet, outside of not wanting to spend his time over-analyzing every decision, he was completely unaware of this internal transformation.

He was, however, acutely aware of how painfully slow time was moving since he'd announced his plans to leave. As a physician, he couldn't give the traditional two weeks' notice, and the two *months* he did give crept along at a snail's pace. He used this time to thoroughly turnover his patients' care, transition out of his role at St. Raph's and wonder how the hell people took two months just to make a decision, let alone transfer to a new job.

Finally, after what felt like an eternity, the Monday lunch meeting with his new team arrived. He joined a group of accomplished neonatologists, most of them new to Sherman as well. Patrick's predecessor had passed away rather suddenly and, because he had been so beloved by his staff, it left an open wound in the department. Patrick's reputation as a hard-driving academic preceded him, prompting several physicians to seek employment elsewhere before he even started. A few others found the management style change too drastic and followed suit shortly thereafter.

These vacancies left room for doctors, like Jay, to move in, seemingly confirming the rumors that Patrick was trying to bring in his own team to replace the existing one. One couldn't argue with statistics though. The fact that he'd recruited 4 new, seasoned neonatologists and a team of nurses and support staff to join the department with only 2 attendings remaining from the original group left little room for interpretation. It was virtually a complete overhaul, and Jay was the youngest member of the new regime, by far.

It was also no coincidence that each of the new recruits had research experience in a variety of studies, none overlapping another. Patrick's methodology aimed to produce new research in several different areas, resulting in an inevitable catapult to national prominence. This made Jay the 'lung guy' in this carefully curated assembly of medical experts.

Working in Sherman University's main teaching hospital, Jay was also charged with the added responsibility of training medical students and residents; a role he was not only confident in but one he would have done voluntarily. Jay found himself surprisingly agreeable to and excited for all the responsibilities outlined in his offer letter. Yet one aspect, whose impact had not been fully detailed at the time of acceptance, was the university's recent alignment with the new Maynard Hospital for Children, which had just received a large endowment from the Maynard estate.

Located in Dayton, roughly 50 miles from downtown Cincinnati, it was still on the cusp of becoming a full-service hospital. This partnership was intended to accelerate the development of the children's hospital while filling a gap in Sherman's current institutional network.

The expanded corporation and available resources suggested additional opportunities to an already exciting situation. Jay now had the infrastructure for inestimable and progressive research, ability to impart his knowledge on a younger generation of practitioners, and potential for career growth at his fingertips. Thus began his tenure at Sherman.

*∗∗

Along with the brash resolve from Jay's youth went the independent mentality of his medical debut. Instead, he made the time and effort to get to know the nurses he was to work with, hoping to avoid the mistakes made with the Joans of the past.

"This NICU is much more active than St. Raph's. I wasn't

expecting that since it's not a children's hospital," Jay noted to the head nurse Monica who was also new to the team.

"Mmm hmm," she replied in tentative agreement. He knew he would have to work to build a solid relationship with the nursing staff. Making one casual observation was unlikely to suffice. Jay realized that he was probably not the only doctor to ever act superior to nurses and, quickly humbling and admonishing himself at the thought, pushed the conversation forward.

"How many beds did you have over at Fairfield?" pressed Jay, equally interested in her answer and getting her to engage in conversation. She looked up from the daily log she was reviewing and seemed to consider the question or, possibly, the *motive* of the question.

"We had 25 beds in the NICU, so this is busier for me too. Add in the step-down unit that brings this place up over 50, and you know we're going to be busy!" she remarked with diminishing skepticism.

"Right! Then take that and add to it the delivery room that St. Raph's didn't have and the active transport system and, well..." He raised his eyebrows and shrugged. "It won't be boring, that's for sure!"

They both laughed in agreement, feeling relieved and bonded over learning that they were not the only ones adjusting to more than a change in staff and scenery.

***

Jay's continued effort into building relationships with the nursing staff began to pay off at the onset. He still had to prove himself, but instead of being incapable until proven competent, he was beginning on fair ground. The lack of tension, doubt and resentment helped ease the long and challenging service days. He found enjoyment in the process of familiarizing himself with the team.

Several months into the new busy day norm, Jay learned that the next liquid ventilation protocol was set to start, and Sherman was slated as one of the sites throughout the country that would be enrolling infants. Jay was excited and anxious to prove that the process could work.

Over the course of the next 6 months, he spent a lot of time preparing with a group of interested nurses and respiratory therapists from his organization. The Sherman team then moved on to working closely with a team from the lead facility in the trials, a prominent hospital in Rochester, New York, to ensure that everything was arranged to give the trial the best likelihood of success. Safeguards were in place. Documentation was reviewed and signed. The company sponsoring the protocol, hoping to prove the technique successful and move on to market it, had been advised of the risks. They were ready for enrollment.

Each facility in the protocol network vetted infant cases, all younger than the previous three he'd studied, which meant less damage from the ventilator to contend with. Every day that passed enhanced the fervor within everyone in the protocol. After a few weeks of screening, a little girl named Adrianna was born very preterm and struggling to breathe. The attending physicians quickly assessed the protocol criteria and checked off every box. Adrianna became their first candidate.

***

"Jay, it's Thomas. I have a newborn girl in here who isn't responding to any of our efforts to help her breathe. She fits the criteria, and I'm sure her parents would give consent—"

"I'm on my way," Jay said, throwing the covers back and dashing towards the bathroom. Pulling a shirt over his head while simultaneously squeezing toothpaste onto his toothbrush, he hurried through his morning routine. Gracelessly, he hopped across the bedroom on one foot, like a drunken rabbit, shoving the other into the leg of his pants. After bouncing off the bed several times before ultimately succumbing to gravity, he finally surrendered to the process and finished getting dressed properly.

He grabbed his wallet and keys from his nightstand but stopped to gently kiss the back of Kathy's head, which was buried in her pillow to avoid seeing the early morning sunlight and hearing his clumsy, chaotic haste. He had truly done his best not to wake her because he knew she was exhausted from covering shifts for a fellow physician who had just gone on maternity leave. Whether the extra hours provided her with a distraction from or reminder of the fruitless efforts to start a family of their own was undetermined. All that was certain was that both he and Kathy were nearing the end of available options to conceive without any of the desire to do so diminishing.

He paused ever so briefly as he nestled into her hair. He knew it would all work out somehow, he just wished it didn't have to be so hard. This was one more reason he needed a trial to work. He wanted to bring home a success, something to lighten the weight of their frustration. He pulled away from her tangle of curls, the smell of honeysuckle lingering on his lips, injecting him with energy. As he descended the stairs two at a time, he heard her call down to him.

"Good luck, Jay! You got this!" She shook her head in proud amusement then dropped back into her pillows, welcoming sleep to return on her first morning off in 6 days.

*****

From the car, Jay phoned the research team and told them they had a viable candidate who had been unresponsive to both surfactant, which was now FDA approved, and the hospital's best and newest ventilators. Each team member reacted with similar degrees of excitement, hoping for a much-needed success.

Jay carelessly ate a granola bar he'd grabbed on his way out of the house, sending oats in all directions as he multitasked in the car. He managed to consume about half of it in between calling the team and navigating traffic before brushing the resulting debris off his shirt and pants onto the floor. The small portion would serve to stave off any distracting hunger pains, and adrenaline would provide the necessary energy.

The upcoming tasks and procedures buzzed in his head as he ran through the process he'd come to memorize over the past months. Pulling into the Sherman employee parking lot, he realized he had no recollection of the drive. He was full of anticipation, walking towards the entrance and, hopefully, a different outcome.

Thomas met Jay in the hallway to further brief him on Adrianna's status. She had not gotten any worse since they'd spoken, but she had also not improved. Their first objective was to obtain consent from her parents who seemed primed to give it, nearly intercepting the form as Thomas passed it to Jay so he could review it with them.

"We know she's up against the odds, so do whatever it takes to help her pull through," said Andrew, vocalizing his consent in the matter-of-fact manner that many fathers use in tough situations. He shook Jay's hand and gave him a short nod in acknowledgement of the severity and risk. His other arm remained wrapped tightly around the shoulders of his wife as if he were the only thing keeping her upright. Or perhaps, he was using her as a crutch for his own sake. Regardless, they needed one another in this moment more than ever.

"Do whatever you need to do, Doctor. Please," pleaded Toni, the mother. She clutched her sweater, bunching the material over her heart, and looked at him with cautiously eager, exhausted eyes that had dried and swollen from the many tears and sleepless nights spent by her tiny infant's bedside.

Jay hated that he was familiar with the sound of a mother's plea, the gaze from eyes full of sorrowful fatigue, the grasp of hands dry and cracked from over-washing just to be able to touch their child's miniature hand or foot. Along with the parents, he yearned for their infant's survival too.

"I promise you I will do everything in my power to help your little girl," he assured, giving Toni a kind smile and comforting squeeze on her upper arm as he handed the executed consent form back to Thomas. "Now, let's get setup," he chirped, moving towards the team that was converging with the equipment. He was followed by Tom and Marla who had recently arrived and been debriefed.

Within an hour, the equipment was assembled and team ready to begin. The beauty of the partial liquid ventilation (PLV) study's design was that it required less prep than the previously used equipment. It also varied in protocol. Rather than breathing liquid into the lungs in breaths, Adrianna's lungs would, instead, be filled with liquid first then breathed on by the ventilator – a very simple idea, if only they could get it to work!

Everyone took their places, ready to execute. Jay genuinely believed in the team and the concept. They all knew what had to be done and in what order. His self-confidence was boosted by having Monica as his assistant. Determined not to duplicate the dynamic he'd contributed to creating with Joan, he had been careful to build strong working relationships with this staff, specifically the head nurses.

To avoid the disconnect and resentment that would result without a conscious effort on his part, he practiced small talk in addition to medicine, which led to discovering shared interests and establishing common ground, ultimately producing a comfortable work environment. At least it had only taken a few trials to get *that* concept to work.

Jay, now intensely focused on his tiny patient, removed the ventilator and began slowly injecting the fluid into her lungs until it started coming out of the tube, indicating they were nearly full. Next, he placed her back on the ventilator to help push the liquid down, adding more fluid as it allowed.

"Eighty percent," reported the saturation monitor, which, in addition to regular announcements, also beeped in unison with the heartbeat, adjusting its pitch to indicate increasing or decreasing levels. This offered providers the necessary data without the need to look at the machine. As beneficial as this feature was, it also risked having a similar effect to the music during final jeopardy.

Ok, 80% isn't too low to survive, Jay reassured himself. He knew that this was much lower than the normal 97% -

100% of a person with healthy lung function, but he also knew it was not low enough to give up hope. He continued injecting the liquid as the beeps became lower pitched and less frequent.

"Doctor, saturations are falling..." informed Monica.

Jay looked up from Adrianna and saw the dread on Toni's face, reminding him of the other 3 trials. *Why isn't it working?!* he thought in exasperation.

"Fifty-nine percent," the monitor flatly declared.

"Vitals are stable, but saturations continue to dip," Monica supplemented. "Do you want to transition her back to the ventilator?" Monica trusted the doctor and wanted to be prepared to support the procedure as best she could.

"Not quite yet," he replied, hoping his voice disguised the apprehension he felt.

Jay did not look away from Adrianna. He continued to observe her response while injecting the fluid.

Come on, little girl. Come on! You have parents here waiting to hold you and bring you home. You can do it... he urged silently. He desperately wanted this to work, for her to pull through. It felt as if the only sound in the entire hospital came from Adrianna's saturation monitor. Beep... Beep... Beep...

The team maintained their individual tasks, observing her vital signs and responses to the steady, low-pitch soundtrack. Time seemed to be standing still. Tom and Marla held their breath, tweaking the flow and pressure of their equipment ever-so-slightly. Beep... Beep... Beep...

"Fifty-one percent."

The monitor mocked them; mocked the years of tedious research, discouraging presentations and trial failures they'd endured.

Come on! Please! Beep... Beep... Beep...

More time passed, dragging the minutes and their hope along with it. Then, something changed in the metronome-like beeping.

Jay couldn't take his eyes off the tube that was feeding the liquid into her lungs, but he heard the difference. They all heard it. Had they heard it right? Was it really raising in pitch? Was the frequency increasing?

Beep, beep, beep... It was! Like the sound effects of someone wandering a dark and dangerous hallway in a horror movie, feeling around for a way out before finally finding an outline of light from the safety of the outdoors, the steady but slow croaking accelerated into more of a whimper, indicating there was still some fight left in the little body they worked on. The pitch continued to climb, and the pace quickened. Frozen in anticipation, they literally listened to the sound of Adrianna's life coming back.

"Sixty-three percent," the monitor asserted, piercing the silence with confirmation of what they were hearing.

Beep, beep, beep...

Color returned to Adrianna's face with every heartbeat.

"Seventy-seven percent."

Marla gasped inadvertently. Tom looked at her with apprehension.

"Eighty-four percent."

The mechanical announcement took a moment to process. They'd done it! They'd gotten Adrianna to a saturation level that was higher than when they'd initiated the procedure! They all knew better than to celebrate just yet, but this was the best result they'd seen to date.

They remained at her bedside for over an hour, administering fluid as her lungs expanded while simultaneously weaning her off the ventilator.

"Ninety-one percent," the monitor reported, and for a brief moment, Jay thought *it* even sounded encouraged by the reading.

Toni looked to Jay for permission to hug him, where, upon receipt, she fell into him, sobbing in joyous disbelief. Jay was happy it had been her to burst into tears because he didn't feel it would be appropriate for him to do so, despite wanting to.

With tear-filled eyes, Andrew guided his wife back to his side before embracing Jay himself.

"Thank you, Doctor. Thank you so much," he managed to say, fighting to control his emotions.

"You gave us our daughter back. You have no idea— You have no—How can we ever tha—" Toni capitulated to hers, burying her face in Andrew's neck as she both wept and laughed.

The outcome of the procedure steeped the room with so much delight, disbelief, encouragement, gratification and relief. While filling Adrianna's lungs with fluid, they'd filled their own hearts with faith and a little girl's body with life and possibility. Their confidence in the hours upon hours of research had been restored, and a family, torn apart by hours upon hours of worry and fear, had been made whole again.

Tom, Marla, and Jay exchanged congratulatory looks, overflowing with exhilaration. Patrick arrived in time for the credits, filled with pride for the entire team. It was not lost on any of them that they were witness to the beginning of something very special. Tom, Jay, and Marla had just become the proud parents of a successful new therapy that now had the *proven* potential to save the lives of infants with lung disease.

But it is no secret that money rules most things. The company sponsored Tom, Marla, and Jay's therapy through another 13 trials, 7 of which were performed at Sherman, before deciding the success rate was high enough, despite it being under 100%. In the interest of recouping the losses from the infant studies, they wanted to move on to treating adults, hoping the increased amount of liquid required would generate more revenue to apply to their accrued debt. This worked in theory but not in the trials, and the company eventually folded.

Regardless, that did not stop liquid ventilation from becoming a niche therapy in nurseries around the world, but the cost of the perfluorocarbons prohibited it from becoming commercially viable. Sure, the amount required for infants was affordable, but the small quantities did not justify the production and marketing overhead expense, yielding only a small margin for profit.

Jay, on the other hand, saw an immense return on investment in the notoriety he received from the studies' success. No longer was there a need to prove himself; his position as a trusted member of the Sherman NICU team had been solidified by the results. This paved a smooth path forward into his career with a determined and vibrant group of providers, busy with the responsibilities of the NICU and the research each continued to pursue.

***

Subsequently, Adrianna was effectively weaned off the ventilator and began growing steadily. Each day Jay thoroughly reviewed the notes from the previous doctor on service only to be pleased with her progress. The reality of the triumph over death became clearer with each status update. She'd become his first stop each shift, a way to begin on a note of positivity and hope. He walked over and found Toni in her usual position at Adrianna's bedside, a permanent suppliant, aching for continued recovery.

The area of the room that had been designated for Adrianna appeared brighter than it really was. The NICU, as a whole, was dimly lit and glowed with a blue hue from the many infants with jaundice lying under the UV lights with miniature sun protectors over their eyes, like a baby tanning salon. It was generally quieter than other floors or departments as well. This dim silence produced a comforting effect just as easily as it could become a setting for sorrow. Fortunately for Toni, it would never become the latter. Adrianna was to be discharged the next morning after a harrowing journey to survival.

"Hi Toni, how is our little pioneer?" Jay asked, grabbing her chart from its cradle, his white coat a bold pillar, supporting so much more for Toni than his role in the room.

"She's good." She smiled with gratitude for those words and the ability to use them in conjunction with her daughter.

"Great to hear. Now, let's see the specifics," Jay said as he began to review her statistics from the previous night.

Satisfied with the information within the notes and his own assessment of the little infant, he spoke with Toni for a short time as he did more often than not. They had bonded, just as everyone in the room had on that miraculous day. Each person affected by the magical experience.

"I've enrolled in nursing school," Toni professed. She laughed nervously, suddenly lacking the conviction she'd had when submitting her application.

"Really? That's wonderful!" Jay replied with sincerity.

"Yeah, I guess. I mean, I just feel like Adrianna's life was a gift, and I want to help give that same gift to other babies, other families, other mothers. Andrew suggested it, actually." She smiled at the thought of their victory over certain defeat, like a kid who'd just learned to ride a bike without training wheels or swim without water-wings.

"I can't think of any better reason to become a nurse or better way to pay it forward," he said understanding the motive. "Maybe one day, we'll work alongside one another."

"Wouldn't that be something? Either way, Andrew and I would like it if we could stay in touch," she half-stated, half-asked.

"Of course! I want to hear all about Adrianna as she grows up. In fact, I wouldn't have it any other way," Jay declared, thankful for the opportunity to remain involved. They had grown close over the course of Adrianna's treatment, and he would miss them otherwise. "Until then, you know where to find me."

Andrew joined Toni for the last hours of their daughter's stay, which were also the last of Jay's shift. When the time came, the victors expressed their gratitude to one another and exchanged contact information. Then, Jay walked the little family to the parking lot where he received all the validation he needed for the journey to this point. He watched two parents do what they feared would never be possible. They took their daughter home.

9

Making Lemonade & Continued Volunteering

If Patrick's leadership of their department ever ended, he could easily find success as a stalwart or lobbyist. His dogged pursuit of getting his team's needs met may not have resulted in popularity with the other leaders, but his advocacy was admired by his subordinates since he did so in support of them. His drive was reinforced by the profitability of their team, giving him no reason not to make demands, often pushing back against the department chairman until he got what he wanted.

Jay admired Patrick's willingness to stand his ground based on his department's proven and consistent success. Jay appreciated Patrick's ability to ignore the social fallout from his methods with executives while remaining motivated and positive about his objectives. One day, Jay hoped to accomplish as much as Patrick had but doubted the likelihood of his ability to generate the fearless tenacity that was the mainstay of Patrick's success. Jay knew he could never be as uncompromising in a negotiation, even if it was for his own team's benefit.

Patrick was tough but fair, available but distant. His

effect created a focused, disciplined environment full of high expectations relayed in a matter-of-fact manner. It was hard to dislike him because he kept himself at arm's length, and his leadership style was not cruel or unreasonable. Rather, it was merely very straightforward. No niceties. No small talk. No elaborate explanations. He simply defined the scope of the objective, delegated tasks and expected results by the deadline. In short, no nonsense.

Consequently, when Patrick called the group together for a special meeting, the team knew a substantial change, opportunity or expectation would be disclosed. Knowing Patrick wasn't the type to drop a bomb on them without warning, there was minimal discussion or projection amongst the team about its purpose in the time leading up to the meeting.

The symbolism of the conference room's transparent walls was not lost on anyone. Patrick sat in his usual place at the table's helm as everyone filtered in and found a seat. The table was bare except for a single water bottle and several cups in the middle, afterthoughts from a prior meeting. Chairs were adjusted, and Jay watched a few of his colleagues set notepads and pens down in anticipation of being given a detailed directive.

Patrick cleared his throat. "Thank you all for coming. I won't take up much of your time, but I want to inform you of some personnel changes coming down the pike." He paused, letting the team dangle for a moment as he grabbed the water bottle from the center of the table and twisted the cap open in one swift motion, breaking its seal.

Jay and his colleagues exchanged puzzled looks that implied interest but lacked apprehension or concern. Several pagers buzzed, alerting the owner to a need that had arisen. However, no one made a move to respond after checking them, so clearly no urgency was required.

"As some of you may already know, my boss Russell Nubinski is retiring as the Chairman of Pediatrics at the end of this quarter. Now, they have not selected a replacement, but I have it on good authority that I have been given the nod."

No one reacted outside of acknowledging receipt of the information. It was far from unusual for a department lead to be next in line for a freshly vacated role, higher up the food chain. Plus, Patrick's ambition had earned him the promotion after cultivating a successful department.

"Similarly, I plan to fill my own role of division chief internally. I called you all in here today because every one of you is qualified to step up."

Jay scanned the room full of nationally known researchers, imagining himself reporting to any one of them. He found no concerns. Each were natural leaders, and after four years, the team, once unsure of one another and the logic of their assembly, had developed a mutual respect and understanding of each other's roles. Despite being the youngest in the group, Jay had accumulated enough experience and acclaim to be considered an equal but not enough to be considered as Patrick's successor. At least not in Jay's opinion.

Patrick sat quietly, waiting for someone to speak up. The announcement followed by his silence spawned a collective shift in seats, averted eyes and weak attempts to feign interest despite the obvious lack of enthusiasm.

"I would really like to fill my position with someone I trust to keep the department progressing at the same pace, which is why I'd like you each to consider throwing your hat into the candidacy ring." He recapped the now half-empty water bottle and slid his chair back to stand. "Think it over and come see me if you're interested." Then he left. No nonsense.

Through the glass wall, Jay watched Patrick stride down the hallway.

"Great. Well, *I* certainly don't want Patrick's job! I prefer smooth sailing at work over going to battle on a regular basis," joked Amy, one of the more veteran neonatologists in the division.

Several chuckles escaped from the nodding heads of the group.

"Well, *someone* has to step up because I know I don't want an outsider to assume his role. We may not be as lucky as we've been under Patrick if that becomes the case," stated Yulin whose research had flourished under Patrick.

"Then have at it because I have no desire for that kind of burden. You're right though," she admitted. "It would be much better if it were one of us."

The team tossed the role around the room like a hot potato. Jay agreed with the reasoning behind the reluctancy to take on Patrick's assignment, but his concern for the direction of the division and desire for it to stay on course outweighed the potential negative associations of being its chief. Still, he sat quietly, listening to the healthy debate amongst his colleagues until there was nothing more to be said. The result was the collective agreement that no one wanted the job any more than they wanted it to be filled externally.

Accepting their impasse, the group dispersed, returning the conference room to its original state, the only difference being the half-empty water bottle at the head of the table, set apart from the cups it would now never fill.

Jay was consumed by his thoughts, which he planned to unpack when he got back to the privacy of his own office; the other end of the hall now seeming to be a great distance away. He flipped on the lights, walked over to his desk, bent to sit but instead, straightened himself, circled back around to the door, flipped the lights off and headed to Patrick's office.

He found Patrick already absorbed in work in the small room at the other end of the hall. Somehow, the countless reference books, medical journals, reports, and other documentation that lined every available surface expanded the feel of its size more than the windows on the exterior side or similarly transparent interior walls. Cradled in the oversized chair behind his oversized desk, looming over everything within the office, Patrick waved him in.

"Hi, Jay. Hang on while I get to a stopping point," he said, holding a finger up, still focused on his computer.

Jay took a seat in a chair designed to provide no more than a temporary resting place. Like its owner, it welcomed you to sit but not stay.

"Ok, there we go. Thanks for waiting. I hate losing my train of thought, which happens enough at my age. I've learned it's best to finish because the chances of picking up where I left off are slim these days." Patrick's lightheartedness quelled Jay's nerves, providing the courage to say what he'd set out to say.

"Do you have anyone specific from our group in mind to move into your position?" Jay inquired.

"Honestly, I don't. I think you each have your individual strengths and weaknesses, but I feel any of you would be a good fit. Guess it really comes down to who wants it."

"Well, in case no one steps forward, I wouldn't mind being considered for the role. I realize I'm the youngest physician in our division, but our group doesn't require much leadership, and there's no need to change any of the processes you've established. Plus, you'd still be leading us, in a sense, so I'd continue to have your guidance as I learn.

"I hope you know how appreciative I am for the offer you made me four years ago. I would be just as grateful if you gave me this opportunity." Jay finished and waited for a response. With every moment that passed in silence, he seemed to shrink in the chair that had not endorsed the duration of the conversation.

"Jay," Patrick exhaled, slightly shaking his head in disapproval. "I appreciate your offer. You made some valid observations, but I have to say…" He adjusted the glasses resting on his nose so that they framed his eyes that were lined with experience, age, and years of departmental arm-wrestling. Jay began to regret volunteering for the position when he knew it was a reach. "I don't have to be desperate to consider you for the role, Jay. When I said that each of you was more than qualified to fulfill it, I meant it. Have I ever been known to blow smoke just to be nice?"

"Good point," admitted Jay, who could not argue that fact. "Well, I just figured…I mean, none of us wants an outsider to come in, but if no one else steps up, I wanted you to know that I am willing to, if you'll consider me."

"Look," Patrick started, removing his glasses altogether and placing them neatly folded into his coat pocket. "I think you'd be just fine in this role. Like you said, our division doesn't require much focused leadership, and we have established processes in place that work well for our objectives. That much is easy. Where I think you will struggle, if

I'm being honest, is when the time comes to stand up for those goals and solicit what is needed to achieve them."

Another good point, confessed Jay internally.

"You have many people behind you who know your competence. You need to become one of us. If you're not confident in yourself, why should anyone else be?" Patrick raised his eyebrows at this redundant, checkmate question. "Somewhere in there," he pointed at Jay, "you know your worth. You believe in your ability, or you wouldn't be sitting here, throwing your hat in the ring. But, if you are to take on my position as chief of the division, you must learn to display that confidence in both your mannerisms and speech. Otherwise, you'll get tangled in all the red tape if you're not eaten alive by the other executives competing for the same dollars as you."

Jay knew that everything Patrick had just laid out was true. He also knew it was meant as constructive criticism, coming from the same place as the offer four years ago; the desire to improve the hospital, the department, the individuals, and the leader driving it all. Patrick could see that his words had resonated with the young physician.

"You've given me much to think about, and I believe I've done the same for you. Let's circle back on this topic tomorrow after you've had more time to think it over," Patrick pitched.

"Yes, I would like that. I appreciate your feedback and hope you know that I share the goal of maintaining the success of our team." Jay stood to shake Patrick's hand, pushing the chair backwards, which made a sound that resembled a sigh of relief, irritated to have been sat in for so long.

"Of course, I do," said Patrick, rising to meet Jay.

"No matter how the cards fall, I won't let you down. I haven't yet, and I don't plan to start now."

"I have no doubts. Keep reaching for things but adjust your approach. You're not afraid to volunteer, so don't be afraid to assert your reasoning."

"10-4," said Jay with a causal salute. "I look forward to revisiting this tomorrow."

"As do I." Patrick fished in his pocket for his glasses, which he unfolded and replaced on his nose before sitting back down. "Oh, and Jay?" he called out, stopping Jay mid-stride just as he was about to disappear from view through the sheer office wall.

"Yes?" he replied, leaning into the doorway.

"Thank you for stepping up. I had a feeling it would be you, and only you, who would." Patrick gave him a fatherly wink paired with a smile that came from the pride of years of mentoring.

Jay smiled back, filling with gratitude for the takeaways of this conversation. He saluted once again then headed back down the hallway to prepare himself to merge back into the day's routine.

***

When the decision was finalized and announced two weeks later, Jay found himself signed up for another unknown journey. He assumed his time would be spent similarly to Patrick's, which was unclear outside of the fact that he never spent much time on service or on call or at the hospital at all, really. Jay wondered what had taken Patrick away so often, considering the possibility that he, too, would be tasked with the same meetings, lectures, and other commitments. The potential for this made him worry about how feasible it would be to continue the research and clinical care he so enjoyed.

Over the course of the months leading up to the transition, Jay met individually with his team partners where they expressed their support and asked that the autonomy granted under Patrick continue under his leadership as well. In discussing the upcoming changes, he also learned that they shared many of the same fears, most centralized around whether the responsibilities of the division chief would consume too much time, hindering his ability to pursue or participate in anything else.

Eventually, the time came for Jay to step into the next chapter of his career, regardless of fears, unknowns or concerns. He navigated each new task with an open mind while trying to find his own management style. After a while, Jay fell into a comfortable rhythm with his administrative team and discovered that decisions came more easily and with less controversy than he had anticipated. Perhaps, this was due to the difference in his approach, which involved passing along information he received from above in an effort to encourage transparency and asking the team for input on what they needed to meet their end goals.

Jay's intent was to establish mutual respect and trust, acting as a servant leader, so the team would feel like he was working for them more than they for him. The result was a culture of appreciation and coordination. With each item they checked off the list, they picked up steam to continue their forward progress.

Despite the NICU remaining busy, Jay didn't have near as many commitments as he had feared, which gave him the time to maintain his research and be on service for clinical care. Conversely, Patrick faced a much more taxing challenge in his new role as chair, which required him to spend the majority of his time at Maynard, helping to turn it into a full-service children's hospital.

Although he only made the rare appearance at Sherman, Patrick made sure to check in with Jay on a regular basis. It pleased him to hear that Jay was becoming comfortable in the role of chief and relishing the additional respect he received from students and freedom to get work done at his own pace, which, in this case, happened to be faster than when Patrick ran the ship.

Jay took the grievances he'd had as full professor and did his best not to duplicate those situations with his team as chief. Documents no longer sat on a desk, waiting for signature approval. Questions were answered promptly and without a reminder. He prided himself in working just as hard, if not harder, than everyone on the team and being visually present in either regard. He paved the way for individual and collective success, knocking down barriers without the aggression or need to fight. By taking the time to find a common ground when a disagreement arose, he was able to cultivate the healthy and pleasant relationships with leadership that Patrick never could (or strove for).

Of the numerous obstacles confronting Patrick, leading pediatricians with more expertise than himself proved the most difficult. As division chief of neonatology, his clinical, educational and research expertise was a triple threat, unmatched by anyone on the team. As department chair over both Sherman and Maynard, his charge covered all areas of pediatrics from general to gastroenterology to psychology. Once the expert amongst experts, the promotion reduced him to being an expert in only one of the 20 specialties he oversaw.

With two hospital systems not only distant in geography but also in organizational culture, he found the deck further stacked against him when the more familiar one began losing its long-standing clout as the focus shifted towards turning Maynard into a successful full-service children's hospital. He became largely viewed as an outsider and, without the leverage of a successful department, Patrick's management technique of pressure and insistence produced few desired results and many objections from the more profitable ones, such as surgery and orthopedics.

It was hard to hide his mounting frustration and the stress he was under. Rather than adapt to a new leadership style or work towards a coordinated approach to achieving his goals, Patrick decided to move on from the organization after just two short years as chair. Jay was sad to see his mentor go and wondered if, perhaps, Patrick had so much valuable advice to give because he hadn't taken much of it for himself.

***

Jay and Kathy sat in the waiting room of the adoption agency located in an old Victorian house that had been converted for business use. In between pairs of worn Queen Anne chairs, end tables offered magazines that were, surprisingly, current. Plants pocked the remaining empty spaces except for one corner that housed a small table and chair next to a bin of toys. Lining the hallway outside of each door were white noise machines set on low to enhance the privacy of the conversations within.

The high back of Kathy's chair remained untouched as she perched on the edge of the seat cushion, clutching the purse that rested on her knees. Jay made use of the Queen

Anne's offer, folding his hands into his lap while resting his elbows on the chair's arms. They were ten minutes early for their appointment by design.

The entire experience that lead up to this point had been an emotional roller-coaster. The past nine months had especially taken a toll. Kathy's miscarriage on the heels of numerous negative pregnancy tests ended their willingness to weather any future attempts at pregnancy. They simply couldn't endure another devastating let down.

They'd moved toward adoption since it fell in line with their shared interest of saving people. So, with the assistance of the agency, an ad was placed in newspapers across the country with a number listed to a separate phone line they'd set up to take any calls in response.

For months, Kathy manned the phone, trying to persuade countless mothers not to have an abortion and allow her and Jay to raise their child. The process was stressful and not without negative emotional consequences. Here were two people, willing and able to raise a child, pleading with mothers who were either the opposite of one or both. The logic of the situation seemed unfair. However, they pushed ahead, determined to become parents.

"Mr. and Mrs. Greenspan?" called a voice from an open office. Debbie, their assigned counselor, made her way to greet them.

Jay and Kathy stood up, clasped hands and walked down the narrow hallway filled with the whispers of white noise and possibility.

"Hi there," she said softly, shaking their hands, leading them into her office and closing the door. "Please, have a seat." She gestured toward the available options; a couch whose upholstery was equally as distressed as those who sat in it or two ordinary chairs with grey cushioning that offered basic support.

The couple moved towards the chairs independently yet in unison. The large, oval window behind Debbie perfectly framed her desk and provided enough natural light to only require the aid of a single lamp that sat on top of the radiator cover on the far side of the room. Debbie's voice, that seemed to always pass through a smile, complemented the consolatory décor of her office and created a calming effect in a situation that was anything but.

"Well, I have good news. All of the paperwork for baby Jessica's adoption has been submitted to the courts for finalization," she revealed, smiling with the understanding of all that transpired to get to this point. They sat so still, waiting for the other shoe to drop as it had so many times over the course of this process before Kathy broke the silence.

"Can the mother…can Michelle…can she change her mind again?"

Debbie hesitated, maintaining a brave smile. "There is always a chance she could have second thoughts, but usually in those situations, as you know, it is more of an emotional reaction to than a concrete reversal on the decision. Of course, each situation is unique and delicate. In those instances, we advise the birth mother to discuss her doubts with you to determine their realistic nature."

"Yes, but as difficult as it may be for her, it is equally as such for us! Does anyone realize that? At some point I need to know when I can breathe!" Kathy pleaded.

Jay placed a hand on Kathy's back to console her. He was just as fearful for another mother to back out on them or the state's waiting period to allow another long-lost relative to emerge at the 11th hour and dash their hopes.

"I know," Debbie said, genuinely pained by Kathy's anguish. She had been there for Michelle's first wave of cold feet at giving Jessica up for adoption and witnessed Kathy hand the phone to Jay in utter defeat. She had listened to Jay coach Michelle through her emotions, validate her fears and offer many forms of consolation. She noted his concern for both Kathy and Michelle's perspectives, as well as his own, while he talked Michelle through her doubts and remembered thinking that his patients and their families were lucky to have a doctor like him who tried to relate rather than persuade.

"I cannot guarantee she won't change her mind again, but I can assure you that we will find the right fit for you if that turns out to be the case," Debbie said, having nothing more to offer despite knowing it was a very small consolation to those in this situation.

"I don't want another fit!" Kathy threw her hands up in exasperation.

"I know you don't. But I'm hopeful it won't come to that. You've done so much to get to this point," Debbie began. "Michelle is due in 3 weeks then it's only 3 weeks after that before the adoption is finalized. It's an emotional time for everyone involved. But you're almost to the finish line—"

"Look," interrupted Jay. "We will do whatever it takes to bring Jessica home to us. We're so close and 100% invested."

"That much is apparent," Debbie agreed. "Let's review the paperwork that has been submitted to ensure there are no last-minute questions on your end and cross any undesirable bridges if and when we come to them. I know you're scared, and you have every right to be, but we are almost there. You're almost parents!"

Kathy looked to Jay who encouraged her to stay strong for just a little while longer. Then they went through the motions to finalize Jessica's adoption, all the while hoping that no more obstacles would surface. On their way home, Jay tried to further allay Kathy's unease, finally getting her to where she usually had to get him; focusing on what could be controlled.

They stayed the course, talking with Michelle daily, and things seemed to be moving according to the plan. Until something changed everything, almost overnight.

Two weeks had passed since their meeting with Debbie when they received a call from an OB friend at a local hospital who had just delivered a baby boy whose college-aged mother felt unprepared to raise. They could not believe their luck. Jumping on the opportunity, they brought baby Dan home from the hospital and less than a month later, he was all settled in with his new parents and his adoption finalized. A seamless process, for once.

Three weeks after that, Michelle gave birth to baby Jessica and, although she wavered on her decision a bit, she ultimately gave her child the opportunity to be raised in a comfortable life by two loving parents. Inadvertently, she had also given Jay and Kathy an opportunity they would forever be thankful for.

After years and months of devastation, defeat, frustration and perseverance, Jay and Kathy had become parents to two healthy children within weeks of one another. Now, they could pursue both their career and personal missions – to care for others.

10

Leveling Up & Repeating History

Phil was a successful pediatric gastroenterologist before being selected as Patrick's replacement. Jay didn't know him personally since he came from the Maynard side, and that didn't change much after Phil became chair because the Sherman-specific issues, like the education of its medical students and managing of its pediatrics department, were out of his comfort zone. Because of this, Phil decided to name Jay Vice Chair of Pediatrics with the task of managing the issues at Sherman. Although he was flattered, Jay knew that this promotion stemmed more from Phil's fear of the unknown than as an acknowledgement of Jay's achievements.

Rather than offer it, Phil had, more or less, assumed Jay would take the new position based on Jay's reputation of saying yes to new opportunities. But it did not matter whether it was an option or mandate, the outcome was the same. Jay accepted and enjoyed his new role even though it added little to his resume or bank account. He saw it as a way to ensure Sherman's trajectory while remaining busy enough to limit his availability to interact with the team at Maynard, including Phil, who he had heard could have a temper. Jay simply wanted to maintain a steady course, under the radar, and carry on as independently as possible.

Thankfully, the assignment changed little about Jay's responsibilities. Many of the specialists in Cinci were moving into the Maynard pediatric footprint in Dayton, reducing Jay's charges. He adapted quickly to the role that only added a handful of meetings to his agenda but exposed him to a whole new level of leadership at both hospitals. Jay viewed this new position as a gift that would set him up as the heir apparent to the chair should Phil ever move on. Using the techniques that had gotten him this far, he continued to hone his managerial skills while maintaining focus on his academic endeavors in preparation for that potential.

***

At home, Jay received another assumed promotion to assistant potty trainer once the kids were ready to leave diapers. He and Kathy had effectively charted the unmapped course of having two babies while managing their individual responsibilities at their respective hospitals. It was no small feat, but they tackled it together, leaning on the support of their families when necessary.

Dan and Jess had already brought so much joy into their lives, and parenting came naturally to Kathy whose nurturing instincts were guided by her medical training. This enabled her to offer her children a warm embrace and a level head. Jay loved fatherhood as well. Although the kids were in a stage where they preferred Kathy the majority of the time, he still found ways to bond with them. The simple act of a bedtime story or lullaby provided a solid connection, deepened by repetition. Another valuable lesson from his father.

Other than the obvious and typical changes becoming a parent spawns, the most glaring for Jay was the transition from sympathizing to empathizing with the families of patients. Having children of his own added another element of understanding to the fear and sorrow felt by the families of sick or injured children. At times, the fear of losing them could be so intense that it was hard to override it with rational thought.

Of course, like many parents, Jay pushed this worry down to give way to normal, everyday function. But, as a neonatologist, Jay had to work a little harder than most fathers to push the standard concerns aside. And, after the obstacles that he and Kathy had hurdled just to become parents, it took even more effort to keep them in place.

***

Over time, Jay found his stride as vice chair, tackling the issues that arose at Sherman and Maynard with a growing confidence rooted in proven success. Similarly, he'd also gotten his bearings at home as a father. He resolved dilemmas in pediatric departments by day and helped with homework at night. The established balance of work and family life required constant maintenance, as did home ownership and the many other responsibilities of adulthood. Fortunately, Jay and Kathy worked well together, and neither was afraid of a challenge. This was illustrative in the relatively smooth life they had built together.

After nine years in the semblance of a routine, their cadence was disrupted once again when Debbie called. A baby boy, due the next day, needed a home, and she wanted to know if they knew anyone who would be interested. Jay, wanting to help, offered to ask around and get back to her since he couldn't think of anyone off the top of his head.

Later that evening, once he and Kathy had settled down from the day's responsibilities, he mentioned Debbie's phone call and asked her if she knew anyone looking for an adoption.

"Yes! I do, actually!" she blurted out with an unexpected intensity.

"Oh really? You know someone?" Jay wondered, having no recall of her mentioning any of their mutual friends in that situation.

"I do!" she exclaimed.

Jay was confused as to why she wouldn't just tell him who it was. "Great, Kath," Jay said sarcastically, growing a little impatient with the conversation. "Who is it then? Who wants to adopt?"

"I do, Jay! Me! *I* want to adopt the little baby boy!"

For a second, he thought she was kidding and began to laugh. When she didn't join him, he realized she was serious. Very, very serious.

"You want us to adopt the baby?" Jay asked rhetorically. She nodded with a bright grin on her face. "You...want us...to adopt the baby."

"Oh, Jay! Dan and Jess have been such blessings, and I love being a mother. But they're getting older now, and I miss having a little one to care for. I know I have space in my heart for another. Don't you?"

Jay rubbed the back of his neck. "It's not about my capacity, I'm just shocked is all. I didn't know you wanted another child. At least, not badly enough to actually adopt again."

"Honestly, I didn't know either until you just mentioned it. But yes, I do! I really, really do!"

"OK then. It looks like we'll be headed to Babies 'R' Us tomorrow."

She threw her arms around his neck and cried with joy. Jay had yet to fully absorb the decision that had just been made but felt a strange sense of calm and happiness fall over him. He phoned Debbie to inform her and make the arrangements as the thought slowly filled him with excitement. Time for another transition.

As the Greenspan family of 5 shuffled and began settling into their new normal, the Maynard family organization prepared to do the same after Phil announced that he would be moving up to become one of three CEOs, leaving a vacancy in the rung above Jay. Time for another transition.

***

The grueling interview process commenced, revealing characteristics and relationship dynamics otherwise subdued. Jay competed as well, leveraging his esteemed academic achievements to win, only marginally, against the otherwise equally matched candidates. However, in order for a children's hospital to grow, academics needed to be a focal point, and that was as commonly known in the industry as Jay's research.

Before making it official, the two met in Phil's office to hash out the details. With little décor or personal touch, the office left little to do other than getting to the point of being there in the first place. At the suggestion of a few colleagues, Jay had prepared for a tough discussion and little reward.

"What would help make you successful as Chair of Pediatrics, Jay?" Phil inquired, prompting the onset of negotiations. It was understood that a promotion of this degree came with a package. So, like a couple attending a wedding with a cliché playlist, Phil and Jay took to the dance floor as Etta James belted her relief.

"I only have a few asks, honestly," replied Jay, letting Phil lead. He knew that packages could include signing bonuses, promises of new equipment, or the freedom to build a new team of doctors.

"OK then, how much are you looking for?" Phil asked, assuming the direction of the conversation.

"Well, I would like to recruit one of my colleagues at Sherman to continue our work here at Maynard along with a small, renewable slush fund to sponsor lectures and expand research efforts."

"That's it?"

"That's it."

Phil sat back in his chair, grinning like a salesman who just made a sale without having to haggle.

"Alright then! I will happily grant you your requests. You're sure you don't want to discuss a raise or bonus?" Phil followed with, hesitant to believe that Jay truly had no more expectations.

Jay knew he should, or at least could, ask for more money. He'd taken several courses on negotiation while getting his MBA, yet none of the strategies or tactics had stuck. This had less to do with his retention ability and more to do with his distaste for negotiations since many resulted in the breakdown of working relationships, a situation Jay avoided if at all possible. He'd watched Patrick enough to know the fallout.

"I expect to be paid at an appropriate level for a department chair, but I'll leave the determination of that amount up to you," stated Jay.

"Fair enough," assured Phil agreeably. "Consider it done. Everything you asked for. Done."

Jay left the meeting content with the outcome, honored to have been given the opportunity. He also felt as if Phil's reputation may have been a bit exaggerated because neither the negotiation, nor the overall interaction, had been difficult or tense at all. Because of this, he wished he had approached the meeting differently. Perhaps he would have felt more comfortable discussing a specific raise or bonus if he'd not assumed Phil's reaction. He made a mental note not to judge based on hearsay in the future.

Regardless, Jay was satisfied with his new assignment. And although he had to relocate to the Maynard hospital, he felt otherwise prepared for the next level of challenges. After all, he had over a decade of leadership experience running a profitable department at Sherman. However, had he taken a moment to zoom out on the foundation being laid, he would have noticed certain parallels to Patrick's build and, possibly, tempered his confidence before plowing full steam ahead.

***

The office allocated for the Chair of Pediatrics was a blank canvas waiting for Jay's touch. He unpacked his belongings and personal effects, transforming the office into a professional yet welcoming sanctum adorned with research recognition, reference books and journals, career achievements, his own publications, and photos of Dan, Jess, Justin, and Kathy in a variety of settings and seasons.

His first and highest priority as chair was to remedy the fiscal disrepair of Maynard's pediatrics department. Unlike its Sherman counterpart, it lacked an economic or academic infrastructure, making it critical to begin functioning like a business, enforcing fiscal discipline and operations. Since expanding into a full-service children's hospital, expenses had increased and could no longer be sustained by the trust of Maynard alone.

Jay, coming from an academic institution with a prosperous track record, reviewed the financial statements and was sure he could do better than his predecessors. Blinded by ambition and conviction, Jay walked down the path blazed by his old mentor, similarly unaware of the hidden land mines buried underfoot.

The first explosion came rather quickly. After meeting with several division chiefs, Jay, like Patrick, promptly realized he was in over his head. Coming from hospital-based neonatology with no experience as a specialist working in clinics rounding on patients admitted to the hospital or performing procedures in an operating room, he was unable to benchmark the expectations for each department and assess the effectiveness of their chiefs, a primary task of his new title.

How could he improve their profitability when he had no way to gauge whether he was being fed excuses or accurate information? It *was* possible that the clinic space was, in fact, too small or that they truly lacked the necessary support staff. And, yes, they tended to focus more on the areas that met the patients' needs than on those that drove revenue, which, in a very competitive region, put them at a further disadvantage. But there was no way for Jay to know if this was convenient truth or the direct result of areas of weakness.

Before he could develop a plan of attack, he was pelted by an endless stream of complaints, like shrapnel from the first explosion. Now overseeing 200 providers and supporting staff, the open-door policy he'd employed while managing his department of 8 became a beacon for grievances and petty issues. More often than not, he'd have someone in his office, carping about something that had been said or done to them only to have the other party come in later on to vent their reciprocated frustration.

Jay rarely had to do more than listen, providing an outlet for the incessant list of issues between his staff. Still, the ever-revolving door impeded his ability to focus on the *real* issues needing attention. This left little-to-no time for him to continue any research, eliminating another enjoyable element of his past position.

Exhausted by the constant buzz of dissatisfaction and overwhelmed by the tasks at hand, Jay wished he'd been more assertive in his negotiations with Phil. Although he'd gotten a fair salary increase, he hadn't been able to move his research support over, and the slush fund he'd been granted was an illusion. Since he created his own budget, he could have easily allocated that amount of money without approval.

The noise from his open-door policy prompted a close working relationship with the human resources department that frequently resulted in Jay's participation in a disciplinary action or termination. And, similarly to the uncertainty around his ability to accurately evaluate the division chiefs, he never felt fully confident in where the blame fell amongst the complaining parties because he couldn't trust the information.

Nonetheless, Jay forged ahead, doing his best to analyze the financials and assess the best way to increase revenue. And, as he finally began making headway and his teams became increasingly effective, Jay looked to receive funding for new projects.

Despite being the largest department and having well thought out ideas, he soon realized that pediatrics was the least respected in the children's hospital, which defied all logic. The accolades, support and marketing dollars all went towards the more profitable departments, which coincided with their projects being prioritized as well.

If Jay succeeded in getting his project ideas heard, his stamina was typically extinguished after months of deliberation leading to their ultimate rejection or underfunding. Being unable to get any of the proposed projects off the ground discouraged his division chiefs and undermined his focus in the eyes of leadership. Jay was in foreign territory, having never dealt with multiple failures or issues he could not resolve. He reached out to Phil and other leaders at Maynard several times to discuss the path forward, and, while they listened politely, they simply had other priorities to allocate the limited funds, which made him realize that he would have to get creative to find the financing needed to move forward.

Jay began to regret accepting his position and resent the decisions of the department and Phil's team. He felt as if he'd been set up to fail; any time he was able to get ahead, his effort was stifled. One step forward, two steps back. This frustrated him because all he wanted to do was improve the organization.

While Jay drifted away from the smooth and successful days of the past, Sherman and Maynard drifted apart in their own regard. Phil and the leadership team continued making decisions without departmental input, and since no one, including Jay, felt comfortable enough to confront them, the wedge was driven deeper with each impact. As chair over both locations, Jay found himself in the middle of an organizational impasse between the newer children's hospital and the esteemed teaching institute. Treading lightly, he did his best to bring the two together despite feeling stuck with a limited ability to influence change.

All the while, Phil continued to climb the ladder, which further deflated the matter and left Jay perched in frustration several rungs below. In an effort to improve his own outlook on things and lead the division chiefs to follow, Jay focused on the positives during their weekly meetings. He highlighted the fact that they had recuperated costs, boosting revenue and structuring expenditures. He celebrated that their teams, albeit at a slower-than-anticipated pace, were working more efficiently and continuing to advance.

By routinely emphasizing their progress, Jay revived his own motivation and reaffirmed his efforts to get things accomplished with the team. They began recognizing what he was attempting to achieve and stopped blaming him for the inability to move the bar. Maynard wasn't competing well amongst the other hospitals in the region, and he wanted to change that. And it just so happened that, one of the ladder rungs between him and Phil was vacant. Jay saw this as a way to affect the necessary change, so he decided to reach for it.

No sooner had he announced his candidacy was he called into a meeting with the leaders of the search. The plain conference room had been converted into their headquarters where they could freely wade in the applicant pool, critiquing resumes and conducting interviews.

"We don't want to waste anyone's time, so we feel it's best to just be straightforward. You will not be considered for the physician-in-chief role that reports to Phil. We feel you are making good progress as chair but not enough to warrant a promotion," one of the two informed.

"So, I won't even be interviewed?" replied Jay in disbelief.

"No, I'm afraid not. This decision comes from the top, so there's really nothing more we can do."

"However, if you continue to accomplish things as you are now, you will make a great candidate the next time a position opens up!" the other puppet added.

Woohoo, thought Jay, pretty sure that his face reflected his derisive inner monologue.

"Well, thank you for…uh, your time," Jay said, fighting hard to sound sincere. *I'm not only rejected, I'm not even good enough to be interviewed.*

Discouraged, Jay returned to his office pissed off that he'd endured his overlooked project ideas, under-funded departmental improvements, red tape-tangled attempts at procedural change, neglected requests for guidance from Phil, and now this. He felt ignored, if his voice had even been heard at all. His frustrations spilled over, and the open-door policy he once came to rue became his platform to vent.

11

The Standards of Behavior & Looking in the Mirror

66 Hey, Jay," Mallory said as she popped her head into Jay's office. "I'm headed out. All things are buttoned up with the nurses, and I've briefed the physicians on service. Anything you need from me before I go?"

Mallory was one of the head nurses who Jay had come to rely on. She was rarely in the middle of drama but always in the middle of keeping everyone on task.

"No, thank you. Go have a good weekend," he replied, looking up from the never-ending pile of documents in front of him.

"Thanks." She smiled, lingering for a moment in case something came to his mind. When he looked back down to his work, she said, "See you at the retreat then."

Jay looked up, but Mallory had already gone. He'd forgotten all about the retreat he had to attend next week.

Like I don't have enough to deal with, now they want us to go listen to yet another consultant drone on and on about leadership, Jay thought.

Maynard had a long history of hiring consultants to help change or adapt the organizational culture to meet the needs of the ever-changing environment. This retreat was centered on leadership and developing, what were referred to as, the "Standards of Behavior." The effort was designed to improve the working environment and decrease some of the human resources challenges they were experiencing. Jay had to admit that there were quite a few HR issues needing to be addressed, but the timing could not have been worse. Fresh off the rejection for the physician-in-chief role, Jay was in no mood to improve his process.

"Jay? Have a moment?" Monica asked from the doorway.

"Yes, of course," Jay said, waving her in. "What's going on?"

"Oh, nothing that important, but I was wondering if, on Tuesday, we could have that quick staff review we spoke about?"

"Oh, well if I weren't going to the leadership retreat next week, I'd say yes, but I have to go, unfortunately. Isn't it ridiculous that they're making us go to this? It's not like any huge change ever comes from one of these," Jay began. "They'll probably have us do a bunch of role-playing and situational re-enactments, fill us with substandard catering, give us generic certificates of completion then send us back to work, expecting a change they'll never actually see." Jay chuckled at the recollection of the many futile retreats in the past.

Monica laughed too, knowing that these retreats never fully lived up to their intent or potential but did succeed in throwing everyone off their routine for a few days.

"What's this one on again? Leadership?" she asked.

"Yeah. They're bringing in some guy named Mark to lead us all on the 'Standards of Behavior' or something," Jay answered, rolling his eyes.

"You know they'll have loads of ice cream like usual, so at least there's that!" Monica laughed.

"Oh, I'm well aware! So is my waistline from the last one!" Jay patted his stomach, which didn't quite support his claim.

He and Monica exchanged a few more jokes about the latest and greatest consultant concept before setting a meeting time to review the staff items Monica and Mallory had submitted to Jay a week prior.

"Well, try to make the best of it. It can't make things worse..." Monica said, getting up from her chair to leave.

"You're not wrong," Jay admitted. "Have a good shift."

***

The retreat location offered some hope that the next 3 days wouldn't be a complete waste. Jay drove up a long, winding driveway lined with trees, like a natural tunnel. The sun shone through the leaves, painting Jay's car with polka-dot shadows and light. The driveway delivered him to a bright, wide-open, circular pull-through in front of the mountain resort. Without the tree coverage, the sun seemed to reflect off every surface, including the valet who approached as he slowed to a stop.

"Good afternoon, sir. Are you here for the Maynard Standards of Behavior retreat?"

"Yes," confirmed Jay as he got out of the car and moved towards the trunk to retrieve his bag.

"I'll take that for you, sir," said a bellman who appeared out of nowhere. Jay, pleasantly surprised by the prompt service, handed over his bag then grabbed his wallet and phone from the center console.

"Whenever you'd like your car, just call this number

about 10 minutes ahead of time, and we'll have it here waiting for you," said the valet as he passed Jay a business card with the valet extension neatly printed under the resort's logo.

"Ok, thank you," Jay replied, taking the card and turning towards the entrance.

"I'll take your bag to your room once you've checked in, which you can do up those stairs and in to the right," informed the bellman, handing him a similar card with a 3-digit number that matched the number he'd strapped to the handle of Jay's bag.

Jay nodded and proceeded up the stairs. Upon entering, he paused to allow his eyes to adjust from the bright outdoors to the darker embrace of the large yet cozy lobby. A woman in a crisp uniform stood poised behind the high wooden counter ready to greet him. As Jay walked over, he heard the familiar voices of the other leaders congregating around the lodge-style bar just beyond the lobby.

"Jay! You made it!" Natalie, the Operational VP, called out, smiling and signaling him to come join them.

Once Jay had checked in, he went over and ordered a beer. He was happy that Natalie was part of this retreat, figuring she would make it less painful to endure. Over the past several months, he and Natalie had developed a strong working relationship that ended up carrying over to a personal relationship outside of work as well. In fact, Natalie and Kathy had become friends, almost more so than she and Jay.

The group of 12 leaders mingled until dinner was announced, moving them from the bar to the dining room. The buffet-style dinner was surprisingly enjoyable, filled with an assortment of different food genres. Towards the end of the meal, Phil went to the front of the room and announced the next day's agenda and start times. Before he finished, he was joined by an unfamiliar man, introduced to them as Mark Sasscer, the president and owner of LeadQuest, the consulting company running the retreat.

"I don't know why *we* have to be here when Mark will have his hands full with Phil alone!" Jay whispered to Natalie.

Mark spoke about the goals of the retreat and provided a brief summary of his credentials and experience, which, despite Jay's lack of interest in the event he had to admit, were impressive and extensive.

"Wow, Maynard may have actually found someone who can enact the change they want to see," Natalie whispered to Jay without diverting her eyes from where Mark and Phil stood. Listening to Mark describe the previous challenges and successes of his company, Jay agreed that the potential for change seemed to be there.

"Guess we'll find out bright and early tomorrow, won't we?" Jay remarked, raising his glass in mock-cheers.

***

The next morning, everyone assembled inside the large, carpeted meeting room, carrying their coffees and items from the extensive continental breakfast. Mark wasted no time getting started shortly after they all settled in. Notepads and pens, embossed with LeadQuest, were placed in each of their assigned seats. Mark welcomed them to the retreat once again then called their attention to the day's agenda, which was found under each notepad. As Jay would come to learn, Mark wasn't one for pleasantries, preferring to get right to business. Jay made a mental note to drink at least one cup of coffee before the next two mornings' sessions even began.

There were 10 Standards of Behavior outlined to the group.

1. Be in the Moment
2. Be Authentic and Humanistic
3. Volunteer Discretionary Effort Constantly
4. Model High Performance – Desired Behaviors that Drive Desired Results
5. Respect and Leverage Separate Realities
6. Be Curious versus Judgmental
7. Look in the Mirror First – Be Accountable
8. Have Courageous Conversations
9. Provide Timely, Clear and Specific Performance Expectations and Feedback
10. Teach, Coach and Mentor – Spend at least Half of Your Time Developing Others

As Mark elaborated on each Standard, Jay could not help thinking how effective it would be if all the leaders adopted these behaviors.

It'd be nice if my separate reality were leveraged even once! Jay thought, looking around the room at the various reactions to Mark's descriptions.

"Jay? Jay?" Mark's voice broke Jay's internal monologue.

"Hmm? Yes?"

"Seems to me that you may agree that change needs to occur?"

"Yes, I do."

"But not within you, though, right?"

"I'm sorry?" Jay replied, confused by the gentle manner in which Mark had basically called him out.

"Well, I see you looking around the room. That tells me

that you find the information applicable but only to others."

How the hell did he gather all of that by me just looking around? Jay wondered, shocked at both Mark's accuracy and audacity. *I'm the one who's tried to improve the department and move up the ladder only to be denied without a chance or solid reasoning.*

"I'll take your silence as a yes," Mark commented before continuing. "As physicians, many of these Standards of Behavior become even more critical to the success of your organization. I'm sure all of you can easily recall a time when you focused on the being in the moment or remaining engaged with the issue or task at hand rather than looking ahead to a solution or back at the cause."

Many of the leaders, including Jay and Natalie, nodded their heads in agreement. Jay, specifically, recalled the moment when Billy had been brought into the hospital all those years ago. He had definitely been in the moment then, no doubt about that!

"Does anyone have an example of when they were purposefully authentic and humanistic?" Mark paused, resituating the cuff of his sleeve while waiting for a volunteer. When one didn't surface, he added, "This is when you focus on communicating with genuine emotion and consider the effect from a perspective outside of science or medicine, in the case of a patient or what have you. But this can also be applied to situations in many, if not every, facet of life, from your relationship with your spouse to that with your boss.

"If we remain in the moment, it aids us in being authentic and humanistic in all that we do as it keeps us grounded in the now." Mark paused once again to allow the information to saturate. "I'm going to pair you off and give you different scenarios to work through," he explained before doing so.

Here we go, thought Jay, wondering if he had rolled his eyes in his mind or in reality.

The groups worked through their scenarios, pausing at the prompted times for self-reflection to pinpoint the moments or areas where the Standards should have been applied to improve the interaction. Throughout the exercises, Jay identified several situations where he had failed to be in the moment or at least be as humanistic as he could have been. He recalled the times he'd gotten consent for the liquid ventilation trials and wondered if he had been too focused on getting to the procedure, perhaps neglecting to be in the moment, which just so happened to be a parent signing off on a gamble with the life of their child.

As Mark described each Standard, he had each department chair work through them aloud. Jay was called on to discuss the 8th Standard – having courageous conversations, which he openly admitted needing to improve upon. He had always been uncomfortable with conflict whether it was advocating for himself or providing constructive feedback, especially laterally or up in the organization.

While Jay listened to the others confess their own areas of weakness, he made a mental contribution of additional ways they could improve their leadership behaviors. Jay believed that, with the exception of a few Standards, he was ahead of the game and certainly ahead of the others when it came to leadership. After all, he was well-respected and had the support of many within the organization, so the problem wasn't *his* behavior. *Right, Dad?* The biggest problem, according to Jay, was the fact that Phil and the rest of leadership made empty promises, rarely following through or making an effort to help him grow within Maynard.

The next two days were filled with more games, role-play and collaboration. Jay found Mark's leadership Standards more helpful than he thought possible. And despite Mark using Jay as an example or putting him on the spot more often than Jay liked, he had confidence in the process and hope for its execution. He no longer felt as if the retreat had been a waste of time, which was encouraging, considering so many often were.

Mark gave everyone "homework" to do before the second retreat, and although the change wasn't blatant after returning to the hospital, Jay noticed that Maynard found many different ways to remind them of the Standards of Behavior, and all the associates began speaking the Standards' verbiage regularly. It was clear that a change of some sort was taking place.

**

The second retreat turned out to be even more of a learning experience for Jay than he had anticipated. Sure, he knew he struggled with certain leadership aspects, but not so much to warrant being, what felt like, constantly singled out by Mark. Although, to be fair, Mark did emphasize that many leaders, including the others in the room, needed to focus on the 6th and 7th Standards of Behavior as well – Being Curious versus Judgmental and Looking in the Mirror/Being Accountable.

"I purposefully spend a long time going over these two behaviors because they seem to be the most difficult to form habits of. This is true for this group as well as many, many others I have coached. It is so easy to play the victim and hard to be introspective and identify your contributions to the problems." Mark paused to gauge the group's reactions. "Jay, do you disagree?"

Jay fought hard not to roll his eyes in mock-surprise at being called on once again.

"I don't disagree entirely, no. But I do feel that there are certainly times when one person truly is the problem," Jay admitted more aggressively than intended. *Like when I propose ideas to advance the Pediatrics Department, but Phil and the others barely entertain them because they're so focused on the surgery or orthopedics cash-cows.*

"I can understand why it can seem that one person is the sole cause for an impasse, but that is likely due to your lack of accountability and looking in the mirror in that situation. Just as in a marriage, there are two people contributing to its success or failure. It's not always a quick, simple truth either. But I assure you, there is always mutual culpability. It may be imbalanced, but no one is ever a victim, and playing one won't get you to the results you seek.

"Let me ask you this…When you're faced with a coworker or boss who is being unfair, in your opinion, how do you handle that? What is your approach?" Mark looked right at Jay who seemed to be hoping this was more of a blanket scenario than one aimed at him for a response.

Jay shrugged his shoulders. "I don't know. Ask for the reasoning behind a decision that you disagree with to get an understanding of where they are coming from, I guess?"

"That's a start, but how likely will their answer resolve your frustration?"

Unlikely because it's never a good reason or one they'll admit to, thought Jay before saying, "Well, you can't really do more than that, so you just have to get over it." *Or at least shut up about it, or you'll never get anywhere with them.*

"That right there is why we are all here today - the defeatist, victim role that we all fall into when we don't get our way. It's a cop out, plain and simple. Look in the mirror and ask yourself why they might have made the decision or taken the action that you feel is wrong or unfair. Ask yourself what role you played in guiding them towards it. Have you always been straightforward with them? Always towed the line...happily and willingly? Have you always had your ducks in a row or game face on? I'm willing to bet that if you asked yourself some tough questions, really searching for your part in the problem, you'd find those answers. That's just part one though. Part two is owning them!"

There were a few mumbles and head nods from around the room, which, internally, made Jay dig his heels in deeper. He simply didn't see how it was possible that he could have a role in every single frustration he experienced at work. *How the hell is it my fault that Phil is a preferential leader?*

Jay hated to admit that Mark was probably right, though. He didn't want to think that he had some fault in the matter. But Jay also wanted to grow within his organization, and whether he liked it or not, Mark knew his stuff. He could easily see how the 10 Standards of Behavior would vastly improve the Maynard culture, but he hadn't really thought about his own contribution to its need for change.

12

Principled Leadership & Embracing Feedback

O ver the next several months, Jay worked very hard to apply the 10 Standards of Behavior habitually, which turned out to be a challenging task. After the retreats, Mark led regular sessions at the hospital that were shorter and more individualized, and Jay had come to look forward to these even though he usually ended up feeling vulnerable and frustrated with himself for not coming to certain realizations sooner...and on his own. Regardless, Jay, with Mark's guidance, began uncovering many areas of his own leadership that needed improvement.

The one-on-one consultations took place in a small conference room one floor down from Jay's office. Physicians used this room when difficult news had to be delivered or difficult decisions needed to be discussed with a patient's family members. It was furnished in a more comfortable way than standard conference rooms, with two couches opposing each other and two armchairs doing the same with a coffee table in the middle. There were several plants scattered around in the corners and on the small end tables, which also held lamps for more intimate lighting than the fluorescent bulbs in the rest of the building. Mark was seated on the couch facing the door, resting his coffee cup on his knee. Jay chose the other couch, swinging his feet up onto its arm and folding his hands on his chest as if in the midst of a therapy session. Mark dove right in, and Jay reciprocated by providing several specific scenarios he felt he needed coaching on.

"Jay, you have to lead by example. If you want your staff to display certain behaviors, you must practice them yourself," Mark replied to Jay's complaint about his backfiring open-door policy. "What resolution do you provide by simply listening to someone complain about someone else?"

Jay said nothing for a moment, thinking about the question. "Well, I thought I was providing a safe environment for my employees to vent their frustrations and work through the issue, using me as a sounding board," he offered.

"All you're doing is providing positive reinforcement to people for complaining about their colleagues. Sure, venting is necessary but not up the ladder and certainly not when nothing productive results from doing so."

"So, what should I be doing instead?"

"I was going to ask you that very same question," Mark replied, forcing him to pause and think, a trait Jay hated and loved at the same time. This always pushed Jay to consider things outside the box more than usual, which was not always easy to do.

"I suppose I could tell them to speak directly with the other person to work towards a resolution," Jay suggested with little confidence.

"That's a good step in the right direction, but don't you

think those moments are great opportunities to coach? As a leader following the Standards of Behavior, you should be coaching or mentoring 50% of the time, and this is a great scenario for that! If you just sit and listen, you're not helping anything. Next time someone walks into your office with a complaint, sit, listen *and coach* them to have a courageous conversation with the other individual. *Then,* when you follow up – because all good leaders do – you can either sit and listen to the progress that was made or provide more guidance towards reaching the solution."

"You're right. Sounds like I struggle with courageous conversations whether they're mine to have or not!" Jay joked in humble admission.

"I won't argue that! Start by asking yourself how *you* handle situations with others who frustrate you and such." Mark raised his eyebrows at Jay, prepping him for feedback. "You do the same thing as your staff! It's called triangulation, Jay, and you default to it when you're unhappy with your leadership. I've seen *and* heard you do it on numerous occasions, in fact."

"What? What do you mean, triangulation?"

"Person A talks to person B about person C. Triangulation. In other words, when you're mad at Phil, you vent to Natalie or Monica or even me! How is that productive? How is that setting a good example?"

"Well, shit." Jay looked at Mark as if Mark had just opened a locked box with the very same key that wouldn't work for him.

"Yep. Not only does that behavior violate the 4th Standard of modeling high performance, it completely ignores the 8th one of having courageous conversations."

"I...So..." Jay trailed off, staring at the ceiling. Mark was right, and there was no way around it.

"Listen, have you ever actually expressed your frustrations to your leadership in regards to feeling like they never give you anything you ask for?" Mark was fairly confident he knew the answer. "I get that people hesitate to have courageous conversations with upper management, but often, the reality is that it leads to results, even if that's just in your own personal and professional growth.

"It's far more powerful to approach management to see what more *you* can do to achieve the desired results than to play the victim who didn't get what they wanted. If you were to ask, you may be offered feedback that could help you reach your goal the next time. Feedback is always a gift that should be embraced, not avoided. Remember, it's about progress, not perfection!"

Jay chuckled when Mark said that last part because, no matter how many times he was reminded, it always seemed to ground his expectations.

"Well, it's obvious that I have quite the journey to make," Jay acknowledged. He swung his legs back into a seated position and rubbed the back of his neck while sorting out his thoughts and next steps.

"Don't worry, you won't be a pain in the ass forever," Mark winked at him then reached across the coffee table and clapped him on the back. The two men had formed a comfortable mentor/mentee relationship, which Jay had come to depend on.

"Good to know there's hope!" Jay laughed, looking up at him. "Until then…" he added as he stood up to leave the session and return to work.

"Until then, I'm here to help," Mark smiled.

***

As the years progressed, Mark took on the role of Jay's informal coach beyond the confines of the Maynard objective, helping Jay learn to use the Standards of Behavior as a backbone for everything he did to move the organization in the direction he wanted it to go. Jay began to embrace feedback, realizing how imperative it was to effective leadership. By holding himself accountable, he was forced to have more courageous conversations, many of which were in the form of providing tough feedback when coaching his young faculty interested in climbing the leadership ladder themselves. Jay offered training, coaching and mentoring, following the 10th Standard of spending half his time developing others. This came easily to him, and he found great joy in doing so.

Some of the division chiefs under Jay were young leadership superstars, particularly the clinical director of the PICU, Claire Ludlow. So, when the chief of the PICU stepped down, and Jay had to fill the role in the interim, he chose Claire. She reluctantly accepted but asked that she be considered for the permanent position, which Jay had no problem with.

As Maynard searched for the best possible candidate to fill the PICU chief role, Claire jumped into the interim responsibilities with both feet while also maintaining those from her previous role, just in case. Although she was young, she was talented, hard-working, and doing everything Jay asked of her, including taking external leadership training. As the search went on without finding any solid candidates, Jay decided to approach his management and propose making Claire the permanent chief of the PICU.

He arranged a meeting with the physician-in-chief, David Vizza, and the chief medical officer, Mehdi Patel, which resulted in Jay reliving the memory of not being considered for the physician-in-chief role a few years before. He left the meeting pissed off and called Mark once he was out of their earshot.

"So, I went to David and Mehdi to suggest making Claire the permanent chief, and they said she is too young and that this is no time to 'settle on internal talent, needing further grooming'! I mean, come on! We haven't found any qualified candidates, and she's already doing the job and doing it well!" Jay marched down the hall and into his office where he shut the door and began pacing back and forth in aggravation.

"As much as I understand your frustration, how is calling me going to change remove the impasse?" Mark calmly asked.

"Dammit, Mark! It won't, but –"

"But nothing. We've been over and over this. Venting is one thing, but if you want results, you have to act according to the Standards. Go have a courageous conversation."

"I just did! What the hell would you call the meeting I just had?!" Jay's frustration with them not considering Claire was amplified by the recollection of his own rejection. Mark understood this and did not take it personally.

"I would call that meeting a courageous conversation, absolutely. But just because you did that does not automatically entitle you to the results you seek. You know all of this…" Mark sighed in empathy for Jay's frustration. "That was a great first step. Since you didn't get what you wanted, what are you going to do next?"

Jay stopped pacing. A moment passed before he declared, "I'm going straight to the top. I'm going to Phil to hear his concerns with Claire being made chief, directly."

"Great. I definitely think that is the best thing to do at this point. You need to be prepared beforehand though," Mark cautioned.

"Oh, I'm prepared alright!"

Mark laughed, "I'm sure you are. But seriously, you can't go into a meeting with him without a plan."

"I know, but I'm much more confident in my ability to have a conversation with Phil. I won't be pushed aside on this one. I want to understand *why* this decision has been made and what can be done to give her a chance."

"I get that, but you can't control what he says or does, so if you meet with him and he offers you no specific reasons, you will have to accept that and switch your approach. With someone like Phil, you'll get a lot further if you allow him to maintain control, even if it's just an illusion. Leverage his reality."

"Good point," Jay acknowledged, resuming his pacing with less intensity.

"Any thoughts on how to go about that?"

"What if I asked him to give her 6 more months in the interim role to prove herself before launching a search with a talent firm?" Jay proposed.

"That's not a bad idea, but it puts a lot of pressure on Claire to perform, and 6 months really isn't a long time," Mark pointed out.

Jay continued thinking and pacing, rubbing the back of his neck while he searched for a better alternative.

"How about I ask Phil to meet with Claire to coach her on what she needs to work on to be considered for the position the next time it becomes available? That way she'll get beneficial feedback from the horse's mouth." He sat down, pleased with this idea.

"I think that is a very powerful suggestion…for both Phil *and* Claire. Plus, it also keeps you out of the victim role because you are adjusting your approach and proposing a solution to achieve your end goal," Mark reinforced.

"Yep, now I just have to get Claire to be open to it and Phil to agree to coaching her, which, if this request is anything like any of my others, won't happen," Jay said, cynically.

"Don't go there, Jay. That's not only teetering on being a victim, it's also going into the meeting with judgment, assuming a result. That is never good. Go in with curiosity."

Once again, Jay had to admit that Mark was right. He was happy to have his advice, though, and even happier to have him on his side.

"You're right. I will. I'm actually feeling good about this plan. I think it may work. And either way, Claire benefits, which is all I'm hoping for anyway."

"Precisely. Let me know how it goes. I'm interested to hear how open Phil is to coaching," Mark said.

"Let's be honest here. We both know I'm going to call you afterwards, regardless," Jay replied.

"Touché," Mark laughed. "I'm thankful for that though. You got this."

After they ended their phone call, Jay sent a meeting invitation to Phil then got back to work. An hour or so later, his phone chirped with the notification that Phil had accepted it.

Let's see if I can get to a 'yes' this way, Jay thought. *Let's just see…*

***

Jay took a deep breath as he entered Phil's baron office,

which was exceptionally bright at that time of day. He was only slightly nervous beforehand, realizing that most of his idea of Phil was precisely that; an idea. He hadn't interacted much with him one-on-one but had heard that Phil was much more approachable when conversations were held in private because he could relax his tough image when there wasn't an audience around. Regardless, both concepts had yet to be proven by Jay himself, so he approached the meeting with curiosity rather than judgment.

The tactic worked. Not only did Phil provide sound reasoning for not approving Claire for the permanent role, he agreed to coach her so that wouldn't be the case in the future. Before the end of their meeting, he even set a time in two weeks to sit down with Claire for an hour. Jay couldn't believe it.

He spent the next two weeks preparing her for the discussion. Anything he couldn't help her with she worked through with her coach to ensure her presentation was thorough and effective. When the time finally came, she was as ready as she'd ever be. She headed off to meet Phil with an open mind, tossing aside his scary reputation.

Man, I hope he hears her through, Jay thought as she walked down the hallway towards Phil's office.

Despite being busy, it seemed like hours had passed when Claire finally returned. She popped her head into his office before being waved in. She closed the door and stood by one of the two chairs in front of his desk. Jay looked at her, trying to read her face for an indication of the outcome of the meeting but finding none.

"You're killing me!" he finally said. "How did it go?!"

A large grin spread across her face, and she began recounting the conversation, which had resulted in Phil's willingness to allow her to progress into the permanent role of division chief of the PICU! The only kicker was that she was told to ask Jay for a package that would ensure her success, which, after hearing what she needed, meant he had to find a way to provide her with something rather significant. But he was happy to do so. He was happy Phil had listened to her instead of maintaining his stance. He was happy he'd decided to have the initial conversation with Phil. He was happy Claire had received clear feedback as well as the result she'd hoped for. Everyone involved had followed the Standards, and the process had worked!

Jay was happy.

13

Looking in the Mirror & Owning Your Actions

Jay remained happy for Claire as he watched her blossom into a solid leader in the chief of PICU role. However, a key objective of Maynard's was not progressing as well and had begun diminishing the happiness within his own.

Contractual negotiations had come to a near standstill between Maynard and ND Health, an insurance company based out of Indianapolis, which were critical to Maynard's ability to bring in patients from outside their small footprint instead of them all going to the Children's Hospital of Cincinnati (CHOC), the world-renowned institution only 50 miles down the road. Maynard not only needed to increase its patient volume, it also hoped to attract the best doctors to allow for high-end procedures, like organ transplants and cardiac surgeries. Jay saw a way to remedy this by forging a partnership with Sherman, but the deterioration of that relationship over many years offered little hope in success.

Jay felt handcuffed, unable to make any progress towards building a national reputation for Maynard and becoming a more impactful advocate for children's health.

Instead, he watched Phil and the physician-in-chief make conservative, risk-averse decisions that unintentionally impeded any substantial growth. He saw them zig when he would have zagged. Where they settled, he set his sights higher. He knew his ideas were valuable just as much as he knew that he, as department chair of pediatrics, was limited in the ability to impart real change.

The culture of Maynard and the pattern of making decisions from the top down didn't seem to be anywhere near changing its ways despite the relatively successful adoption of the 10 behavioral Standards. People were certainly walking the walk and talking the talk, but the change felt trapped on the individual not organizational level.

Jay continued to propose plans to increase revenue, projects to expand capabilities, and ideas to enhance credibility in their weaker divisions while leadership continued to create challenges for resolving strategic issues, excuses for delaying action, and obstacles for Jay to hurdle. It seemed his relationship with Phil hadn't improved quite enough to gain traction despite the lines of communication softening.

Just as his frustration began to mount, the physician-in-chief (PIC) role became available again. Regardless of the continuous rejection, Jay felt confident that he was the right person to fill the position. Maynard needed Sherman more than ever, and their key to that was him! He was well-respected in the region and knew he could leverage his relationships to foster partnerships with other hospital systems, insurance payers and other industries to drive patient and margin growth. The timing was perfect too!

After over a decade of experience as chair, he'd tripled

the department's size, which made the department more broadly respected than the last time he'd applied. With his many successes and knowledge of the region and organizational goals, he was certain he would be the most qualified candidate both in- and ex-ternally. And there was no way they could say he was too young anymore either! Jay submitted his application and braced himself to go through the search committee's process once again.

Phil had partnered with the head of human resources to lead this committee, calling each of the internal applicants into his office, individually, to describe the process.

"Hi, Jay. Please, have a seat," Phil motioned to the chairs on the other side of his desk. Jay chose the one on the left, figuring he should shake things up since he never seemed to leave with a good outcome for himself when he sat in the one on the right. Phil's office was just as devoid of comfort as it had been on day one, the only change being that Jay no longer feared being there.

"I wasn't surprised to see your application. You've been doing a wonderful job as chair, and I figured you were itching for the next challenge," Phil began. Jay smiled, acknowledging the accuracy of the statement. "However, we aren't going to consider you for the physician-in-chief role."

Jay's mouth remained smiling, but the rest of his face filled with confusion and disbelief.

"Listen, I'm sure you feel ready to advance, but the reality is that we are looking for someone who's a bit more of a strategic thinker," Phil explained, leaning back in his chair, clicking the pen in his hand.

"More of a strategic thinker?!" Jay scoffed. *It's not my fault you disregard any and everything I propose!*

"Yes, Jay. You've been very successful as chair, but your style is more 'throwing a bunch of ideas at the wall to see what sticks' than it is strategic." Phil lowered his air quotes and waited for Jay's reaction.

Jay couldn't believe this was happening again. *Now, I'm being faulted for having too many ideas?!* He sat there listening to Phil continue his, obviously rehearsed, explanation while reading the writing on the wall; he would never be able to advance with Phil as his boss. Even if he'd gotten the PIC role, that wouldn't have changed. The hurdles, excuses and conservative culture would remain firmly in place. The only thing the PIC role could have changed for Jay would have been his authority to open doors and cut through red tape more easily.

"I need to bring someone in who can replace me when I'm finally ready to retire, and frankly, you are nowhere near ready for the CEO role."

"Alright," Jay said, putting his hands up in mock-surrender. "I get it."

"I'm not hammering it home," Phil assured. "I just can't have my successor be someone who lays back in his chair with his feet propped up on the table during a board meeting!"

Jay blushed, wondering which time he was referring to. Jay's mouth formed words that did not match his face or body language. "I appreciate your candor and will withdraw my application. If I can help interview any of the potential candidates, I'd be happy to do so."

"You're more than welcome to go through the process anyway, if only for the experience," Phil offered.

"I appreciate that as well but don't wish to waste anyone's time," Jay said. He fought hard to keep the sarcasm out of his voice, his arms from crossing. *On second thought, maybe crossing my arms is a good idea. It may reveal my frustration, but it will prevent me from giving him the middle finger!*

"Don't let this discourage you. Like I said, you're doing a wonderful job as chair. Keep that up!" Phil encouraged as Jay stood to leave.

"Thank you. I most definitely will," Jay replied. "Again, let me know if there's anything I can do to help," he added before leaving and marching back to his office. *So much for the left chair being better luck!*

Once inside his office, he shut the door, opened the folder in his computer that contained his resume, and began revising it for external submission.

***

Margaret Baker had come from Massachusetts with many of the characteristics the Maynard organization needed. She was a strong academic and former pediatric department chair, herself. Although she did not know the region very well, she would be able to keep things stable as the new physician-in-chief.

She aligned her leadership style closely with Phil's, likely to allow herself time to assimilate to her new role and supporting team. She made very little changes initially, which both comforted Jay and confirmed his original thought that he would have been better suited to grow the hospital and gain national prominence.

Nonetheless, Margaret was a very competent PIC, but the challenges of learning the new role and navigating the other leaders left her without the necessary time to develop relationships and network support to move things to the next level. This furthered Jay's frustration because he knew he had this in spades. His coworkers and division chiefs, who saw the need for better partnerships and growth opportunities, echoed this sentiment. Even so, the organization maintained progress at its slow and steady pace lead by its, now, two conservative leaders.

Meanwhile, Jay interviewed for several intriguing jobs at nearby health systems but found none appetizing enough to make him leave Maynard, despite the constant setbacks. He kept his focus on utilizing the Standards of Behavior to maintain the success of his department, seeing all the opportunities to advance fall by the wayside of the cautious leadership.

***

"I don't know what to tell you, honey. You know I agree with you and think your ideas are solid," Kathy said to Jay while they rearranged the furniture in Dan's room. Since he'd gone off to college, there was no need to preserve the high school layout. "What does Mark say?"

"He says that leadership disconnects present one of the most common and challenging conflicts." He lifted a heavy mirror over the dresser's new location. "But it's not like either Phil or Margaret appear very open to discussion… at least, not enough to breach any topic of disagreement. So, you add that to the fact that Maynard is stagnant in its growth, hampered only by itself, and my hands are tied."

"Right, but I highly doubt Mark would agree with you that your hands are tied. What did he suggest you *can* do?" Kathy asked again, having come to know Mark well over the years. She eyed the mirror, which was hanging at a slight angle. "Surely, he had some sort of advice to give on how to navigate all the red tape. No?" She nudged the bottom corner to straighten it.

"Actually, he told me to ask Phil to be my leadership coach." Jay scoffed as he planted a bookshelf next to the dresser, jolting the mirror out of position.

"Really?! That's an interesting idea," Kathy said, walking over to the mirror to nudge it back into place. "What is his thinking behind it?"

"He says that Phil clearly sees something that is holding me back, and, by asking him to coach me, I will gain valuable information about myself while getting to the root of his intent. Although it's not the most appealing idea, it's actually quite brilliant."

"Yes, I agree. It definitely can't hurt the situation."

"Yeah, what's the worst he could do? Not promote me!" Jay laughed, but Kathy knew this whole situation weighed on him.

***

Phil, it turned out, was more than willing to become Jay's leadership coach, offering to meet with him every other week for an hour. At Mark's urging, Jay approached each session with an open mind and viewed Phil's feedback as a gift, whether positive or negative. Only several sessions in, Jay realized this was long overdue and that Phil was actually a good, likeable person once you got to know him. Had he gone to Phil in curiosity rather than judgment, perhaps he'd have discovered this long ago. Mark was right once again.

Amongst the many things the two discussed in their sessions, Phil pointed out that Jay had a habit of publicly voicing and displaying his bitterness surrounding leadership decisions. Simple things Jay did that he was unaware of, like rolling his eyes, sighing, shaking his head, and crossing his arms, all illustrated his disapproval and disagreement. Phil provided specific examples of this behavior, which really drove the message home. Jay knew that leaders had to be purposeful with their mannerisms and words because everyone looked to them for the appropriate reaction. Although Jay hadn't intended to, he now saw how both his verbal and nonverbal messages undermined Phil.

Phil explained that because Jay's body language was very negative and behaviors consistently challenged his leadership, he wasn't inclined to promote him to the physician-in-chief role. Jay heard Mark's voice saying, "My relationship with you can only be as good as the conversation I have about you in my mind." This hit home on a whole new level for Jay after listening to Phil's perspective. So many of his internal conversations about other leaders, not just Phil, were negative.

"Turns out, I wasn't hiding my feelings near as well as I thought I was. Phil said that he wasn't the only one who noticed it either. He said that others have made comments and references to my reactions too. Apparently, I was the only one oblivious to how I came across," Jay confessed to Mark after one of the meetings.

"As hard as this all may be to hear, aren't you glad you're aware now? This is why you need to practice all of the Standards all the time. They aren't effective alone or even out of sequence. Looking in the mirror will only get you so far, especially if you're not even aware of certain behaviors," reminded Mark.

"You're right. You're absolutely right, and I will own my actions. Another thing that Phil reaffirmed for me is that I am one of the most influential people in the organization, people look up to me," Jay began.

"You have an audience, yes," Mark agreed.

"Yeah, and I'm blowing it!" Jay said, half in jest, half in earnest. "I'm so glad you suggested this. I've learned so much about myself but also so much about Phil and his position as Maynard CEO. For example, many of the decisions I disagreed with weren't even his to make! Instead, his boss Bert Sauer, the overall Penmarche CEO, is responsible for most of them. Moreover, he admitted that he disagreed with and was frustrated by many of the same decisions I was! He just never made it apparent to others.

"I think that was the most powerful thing I learned through all of this because I would never, ever, have guessed that! Seems I have some more growing to do, huh?" Jay said, humbled by all he'd learned as he recounted aloud to both Mark and himself.

"To think about all the other relationships I may have missed out on because I didn't approach them from curiosity…I mean, I could have avoided so many missteps just by asking Joan for feedback instead of assuming her motives." Jay paced excitedly around the room, accentuating the now-obvious shortcomings with his arms as if introducing them on stage.

"Patrick would have been a great person to have coach me! Hell, I even screwed myself out of several bonuses and pay bumps because of this!" Jay was energized by these revelations, running through the laundry list of missed opportunities to improve himself, confident he would avoid making the same mistakes in the future.

"After only these few conversations with Phil, I can now see that his decisions came from wisdom and intentions were for the good of Penmarche. That doesn't mean I agree with them, but it does help to know that he is trying to be an advocate for the organization and his teams. It definitely alleviates a lot of my mounting frustrations. Now, I'm just frustrated that I haven't done this sooner!"

"Alright, Jay." Mark interjected, hoping to bring Jay back down to the ground. "I'm thrilled with your enthusiasm and even more pleased with this outcome! We all have growing to do and always will. It's about progress, not perfection. I'm so glad Phil was open to this and you embraced the feedback the way you have."

"Me too! I've said 'yes' to many things I was unsure of in my life, but this is one I will always be grateful for. I never thought I'd say this, let alone feel it, but I actually enjoy spending time with Phil!" Jay admitted.

"That's great! See what a little curiosity can do?"

"You and the Standards never cease to amaze me, that's for sure," Jay confirmed.

"Keep at it, you're doing great." Jay could hear the genuine pride in Mark's voice, which made him most thankful for finally saying 'yes' to the Standards of Behavior many years ago. Without *that* 'yes' he would be so much further behind.

***

Several months into Phil coaching Jay, Bert Sauer announced his retirement. Jay thought for sure that Phil would naturally slide right into this role and was shocked when Walter Trush was hired instead. Jay didn't know if Phil had wanted the job or had even been considered. He never said anything about it, and Jay never asked.

Walter took over quietly, making few waves and even

fewer appearances. It was business as usual at Maynard; Jay trying to continue making progress and growth within pediatrics, his division chiefs all performing well, and Margaret running a tight-lipped, tight-knit ship. It seemed the Maynard theme of inaccessible leadership remained intact with Walter joining the ranks. Jay was the casual outcast, the ever-approachable man of the people amongst the rigid, conservative executives. Still, things were running smoothly when Phil announced his own retirement a short 5 months later, leaving his CEO position vacant.

"Here we go again," Jay told Kathy over dinner that night. *"Another* change in leadership."

"It really does seem like it's constant these days," she agreed. They sat in comfortable silence for a while, eating their meal, both thinking about what this change would bring. "Do you think--"

"Yes, I do," Jay interrupted, answering the question he was already asking himself. "I think it's totally possible that Margaret will replace Phil, giving me an actual shot at the PIC role…finally!"

"Well, it *is* what Phil said they wanted to line up with Margaret and whatnot," Kathy replied, acknowledging the viability of the transition.

"I wonder if Phil will select his replacement or if it'll be up to Walter," Jay thought aloud.

"At this point, nothing would surprise me," Kathy joked, knowing there was little rhyme to Maynard's reasoning at times.

"For all we know, they already have a candidate lined up!" They both laughed, and Jay raised his glass of wine to meet Kathy's in cheers.

***

The next day, Jay was tidying his workspace on his desk when the phone rang.

"Hello?" Jay said into the receiver.

"Hi, Dr. Greenspan. This is Mary Archer, executive assistant to Walter Trush."

PART TWO

The Interim CEO

14

The Servant Leader & Purposeful Approach

Jay and Mark sat huddled over notebooks at a diner down the street from Maynard. The waitress had long since given up on them leaving any time soon, only checking in on them if they called her over or their coffee needed refilling. They were into the third hour of the second round of refining Jay's bucket list. Their plates remained uncleared so they could pick at the waffles or home fries in between adjustments and brainstorming in the attempt to prioritize the list as well as saturate each goal with the Standards of Behavior.

"You know what would be best?" Mark asked, looking at Jay expectedly.

"No, what?" Jay replied without looking up from his notebook that he furiously edited.

Mark took a sip of his coffee, which had gone cold again. Before he tilted it away from his lips, the waitress was by his side with a fresh pot, ready to refill. She topped off Jay's cup as well, which broke his concentration. He reached for the creamer that she had just delivered and poured some in while stirring. Mark leaned back and watched Jay until he, sensing the stare, looked up.

"What?" Jay said, unsure why Mark looked so amused and suddenly relaxed.

"You know what is probably more critical than us polishing your list of goals?"

Jay took a sip of his coffee and thought for a moment.

"Taking a vacation before the marathon begins?" Jay joked, half-considering the idea as it came to him.

"Well, sure. That's never a bad idea before starting something new like this, but that's not what I'm talking about. You're going to kick yourself for not thinking of it sooner. It's obvious…" Mark had wanted Jay to arrive at the idea on his own, but since Jay's thoughts were still all over the place, he chose not to make him squirm.

"You need to host a quick retreat with the new leadership team to help ease the challenges of this rapid transition and create the best chance for success." Mark had barely finished speaking before Jay's facial expression was also one of amusement.

"Duh!" Jay exclaimed, clapping his hand to his forehead. "How did I not come up with that myself?" He leaned back and swiped a piece of waffle that had become soggy from sitting in syrup for so long. Returning it to the plate, he wiped his fingers on his napkin that was still folded on the table as it had been when they'd sat down.

"I told you you'd kick yourself!" Mark laughed. "Here we are spending all this time scrutinizing your bucket list when we haven't addressed what needs to be done *before* any of that! Don't get me wrong, we absolutely must refine the list, but why don't we shelve it for a moment and discuss the 'before the list' items?"

"So, by quick retreat, you mean…"

"By quick retreat I mean a meal or activity on your first or second day in the role, ideally before though, to make sure everyone is on board with your vision and in the moment for your tenure," Mark explained. "Honestly, Jay, it doesn't have to be anything incredibly formal, but it does have to be off-campus," he added.

"When I moved from St. Raph's to Sherman, many moons and more hair ago, I hosted a lunch with my new team to introduce myself and my objectives so that we could get aligned." Jay ran his hand over his head, chuckling at his own joke. "What about a breakfast?"

Mark raised his eyebrows and smiled. "See? You have always had it in you to be a great leader, Jay!" Mark complimented him, pleased to learn of yet another time when Jay accidentally executed a leadership Standard pre-LeadQuest.

Jay smiled back, and the two men sat quietly for a moment, each inside their own heads.

"I think a meet-and-greet breakfast would be a good idea," Jay confirmed aloud as he thought about where to have it.

"Well, it needs to be more than a meet-and-greet, Jay," Mark cautioned, sitting up in the booth and folding his hands on the table in front of him. He leaned in towards Jay who suddenly realized how serious Mark had become.

"Getting your executive team aligned, that's a given. Your main focus needs to be on creating a unified team that is empowered and supportive. You can disagree behind closed doors, but when you leave the room, everyone must be lock step on all decisions, supporting one another," reminded Mark, maintaining eye contact with Jay as he waited for affirmation. Jay nodded and made a note.

"United front – got it," confirmed Jay, reflecting on his

many coaching conversations with Phil and how impactful that aspect truly is to a team's success.

"Ok good," Mark continued. "That's a key ingredient to a winning team, and it's one I know you can cook. Let's finish combing through the bucket list then outline some topics for this breakfast retreat."

"Sounds like a plan," Jay said as he flagged the waitress over. "I think I'm ready for you to take my plate," he told her, relinquishing the soggy waffle remains. "I keep picking at these, thinking I'll find one that is still edible, but as you can see from my napkin, all I'm doing is getting syrup everywhere."

The waitress chuckled and took his plate. She looked to Mark for permission to clear his as well and was given a polite nod. She never minded when they set up their make-shift office in her booth. They were nice, easy customers who always tipped generously for allowing them to do so.

"Can we get a round of orange juices?" Jay asked with a smirk. Mark shook his head at his friend who could always be counted on for a corny joke. "And we might need the lunch menu at some point too," he warned.

The two men returned to grooming the bucket list in a comfortable, familiar rhythm that they had developed after working together for so many years. Although the age difference wasn't great, their mentor-mentee relationship was one to aspire to. Mark had helped Jay distill his innate leadership abilities by nurturing yet tailoring his predilection for risk while cultivating healthy and effective behavioral skills that would become habitual in his daily life both professionally and personally. In return, Jay had given Mark one heck of a success story to reference to other clients.

They met twice more at the same diner, in the same booth, before finalizing Jay's bucket list and breakfast meeting agenda. It was time to take his mark.

***

The kitchen seemed brighter than usual as Jay refilled his coffee. He'd been up early, unable to sleep, like a child on Christmas morning. For the past month, he'd divided his time at work between transitioning out of his position as Chair of Pediatrics and into that of the CEO, and today, it became official.

Justin sat at the table, eating breakfast and watching his father buzz around in scattered excitement.

"Dad, you already wiped the counters down. Twice," he said, shaking his head in amusement.

"Well, what can I say? I'm excited," Jay laughed, checking his watch.

"And you also checked your watch already, like 30 seconds ago."

"Ya know what?" Jay said in mock annoyance as he swatted the dish towel towards Justin. "Leave your old man alone! It's either wiping counters and checking watches or pacing like a caged animal. Which do you prefer?" Jay had run out of things to keep himself busy until it was time to leave and knew it was obvious. Despite this, he made no attempt to hold still, knowing any such efforts would be futile.

Justin had already lost interest in teasing his dad, having returned his attention to the many text messages that pinged his phone at regular intervals; the modern-day teenage metronome.

"Where's your mother?" Jay asked.

Justin shrugged without looking up from his phone. Jay swatted the dish towel at him again, which landed in between Justin's face and phone but failed to avoid being dunked into the cereal below. As Jay pulled the towel back, milk dripped from it, making a dotted line on the floor.

"Oh look, Dad! Something for you to do!" Justin said, sarcastically.

"Yay!" Jay said with purposefully exaggerated enthusiasm. He wiped up the milk trail then went to find Kathy to say goodbye before leaving for the hospital.

Before he left the kitchen, Justin looked up and said, "Good luck today, Dad. You're gonna do great."

Jay smiled and gave him a thumbs up. *I love that little pain in the ass,* he thought as he walked down the hall.

He found Kathy upstairs, getting dressed for her own day at the hospital.

"Good morning," she said when she saw him collecting his wallet and phone from the bedside table.

"Morning," he said back.

"Well?" She turned to him, eyebrows raised in excited curiosity. "You ready?"

"I've been ready!" He replied at a higher volume than expected, which startled her. He laughed, "Sorry, I meant, yes, I'm ready! I've been up since 5:00! You wouldn't believe how clean the counters are!"

Kathy was a bit confused as to why Jay would have woken up so early to clean the counters but decided not to try to figure it out.

"OK, so I can tell you've had your coffee...Did you leave any for me?" she joked.

"Yes, of course." *Where was a dish towel when you needed it?*

"Alright, so what's the plan then? Is the staff breakfast all set?"

"Yes, everyone accepted the invitation. We're meeting at The Caboose first thing tomorrow morning," he confirmed.

"Oh, not today?"

"No, Mark and I went back and forth on that but ultimately felt it would be best if I went in today and got myself situated," he explained, slipping his wallet into his back pocket and phone into the other.

"That makes sense," she acknowledged while applying the small amount of makeup she wore each day. It didn't take much. Just a few dabs here and there, and you'd never know her age or profession. To Jay, she looked just as young and carefree as she had been back in college.

He stopped behind her, placing his hands on her shoulders and leaned around to kiss her temple. She smiled at his reflection in the mirror, full of pride and happiness for what this day meant to him.

She reached up and gently placed her hand on his cheek, "I'm so proud of you, Jay. I can think of no one more deserving of this position."

He met her eyes in the mirror and smiled with humility. "I guess I'll head over to the hospital. There's nothing else I can do around here to keep myself busy, unless..." The humility in his smile was replaced by mischief and his eyes filled with suggestion.

Kathy pulled away, playfully swatting at him. Where was a dish towel when you needed it?

"Eh, worth a shot," he declared. "But, if *you* ask *me,* you know I'll say yes!" he winked and headed towards the hallway.

"Ask me again later tonight!" she called after him.

"You don't always get a second chance to say 'yes', Kathy!" He'd gotten to the bottom of the stairway when he heard her yell over the railing.

"I have my ways." He could hear the smile in her voice. "Good luck, honey. Go show them everything you can do!"

"That's the plan!"

Her 'I love you' floated down and secured his confidence as he opened the door. "I love you too," he whispered before stepping outside and shutting the door.

***

The moment Walter had proposed the interim CEO position, Jay began running through the various changes he would try to implement. His top priority, before anything else, was to maintain his curious, authentic and humanistic approach, especially given the fact that he was inheriting a whole new team; a team that had already been going through a massive transition, starting with the introduction of a new physician-in-chief, the president of the hospital stepping down shortly after, leaving a still-vacant position, followed by Phil, their regional CEO, announcing his retirement, which had been *temporarily* filled by Jay. This meant that at least one more change was to come.

Of the four team leaders now under Jay, he had a solid, pre-existing working relationship with two: Julie and Natalie. Julie, the Chief of Partnerships (CoP), had catapulted to the C-suite from being the neonatal team's secretary. She and Jay had worked together for the past 26 years. Natalie, now the Chief Strategy Officer (CSO), and Jay had maintained their friendship since their days of leadership retreats and collaborating on business opportunities.

The Physician-in-Chief (PIC), Margaret, was still considered new at Maynard. Despite this fact, she had been given the additional role of Director of Research (DoR), and, while she was very talented and capable of handling either role, combining them while she learned a new health system and region proved to be very challenging. To further complicate things, Jay's interim position as CEO moved him from being Margaret's direct report to her boss, a fact Jay chose not to dwell on in order to avoid diminishing his confidence in building a good rapport with her.

Ruth, the Chief Nursing Officer (CNO), like Margaret, had been tasked with more than what came with her role, having absorbed many of the president's responsibilities upon his departure. However, unlike Margaret, she had not received the title or authority to match the additional expectations. Jay knew very little about Ruth, having minimal interaction with much of the nursing leadership as Chair, but what he did know, was positive, and he intended to ensure she wasn't disgruntled by her current workload and lack of its public acknowledgement.

So, with a brand-new team, a strong working relationship with half of the leaders and confidence in building the same with the others, Jay was very optimistic.

He quickly set up his office, having packed up his old one the previous week. He pretty much duplicated the layout, setting pictures of a younger Jay and Kathy holding baby Dan and baby Jess on one shelf, various group shots from family vacations at various ages in various locations along the spacious window ledge, an older Jay and Kathy holding baby Justin and a more recent shot of an even older Jay and Kathy with their arms around college-bound Dan and Jess, who had managed to corral an adolescent Justin. He displayed his degrees on the wall, which might as well have been mandated in the hiring process, before hanging several news articles and magazine covers that Kathy had framed, reporting on Jay, Tom and Marla's numerous successes with liquid ventilation.

The center of the main wall was purposefully left open for his white board, upon which Jay had written the 10 Standards of Behavior…in permanent marker. This served several purposes; first, to prompt people to question his rationale, thus providing an avenue for a discussion about them; second, to illustrate the fact that many business plans, agendas, ideas, etc. can be changed, but the principles must remain intact; and third, to give himself a laugh whenever anyone tried to erase the board.

"Alright," Jay said aloud to nobody, eagerly rubbing his hands together. "Let's get down to business!" He plopped down into the soft, mahogany leather chair, pulled out his notes from the many transition discussions with Phil and began to write out his assessment of the current organizational habits, focusing on the areas he most wanted to change while planning how to align his efforts with being curious, authentic, and humanistic.

Before Walter had offered this position, even prior to Phil vacating it, Jay had noticed that the allure of Mark's teachings had begun fading within the organization. An important part of maintaining forward progress is consistent reinforcement of the desired behaviors, and with all the leadership changes, that element had been interrupted. Everyone – doctors, nurses, administrators – regressed each time they pivoted with a change.

Every turnover brought various degrees of restructuring and reassigning of workloads, which resulted in longer hours and more responsibilities. Maynard had increased its patient intake but was quickly running out of space to accommodate the trajectory. Leaders, feeling the pressures and time compression, were defaulting to giving orders rather than collaborating with their teams. Fear of more changes had taken hold of the organization that was struggling to maintain the momentum it once had. Jay knew he must do something to quell the rising tensions and return the focus to the collective mission.

If he wanted to move mountains, he had no time to waste, and the first step to doing so was to change the Maynard culture from judgmental and autocratic to curious, authentic and humanistic; a mixture of the 2nd and 6th Standards.

Of the 15 goals he and Mark had identified, one of the first Jay intended to tackle was the declining associate engagement scores. He thumbed through the results. The general consensus, according to the surveys (and water cooler talk), was that people did not feel valued or empowered to do their jobs. With many decisions being dictated down with little-to-no input from those departments affected, Jay and Mark had determined that there wasn't enough two-way communication with leadership. They decided that an essential step towards correcting this would be for Jay to be more visible and accessible than previous leaders – bucket list item #4, which aligned with Standard #4.

"Walk the halls," he traced the words on his list and said them out loud at the same time. Tapping his pen against his chin, he searched the ceiling for any additional solution. Finding none outside of those he and Mark had already come up with – host town halls, distribute weekly status videos - he scanned his notes for the next issue.

Julie is not being utilized to her full potential, he read. *Solid leadership position without confidence in her role within the team. Strong operational management skills, willing and able to perform the additional tasks delegated to her in lieu of a new president, yet no title to support it all.*

He read on through the bullet points. *Natalie is very well trained and respected. Strong strategic planning skills and work ethic, positive attitude and collaborative nature. Is she in charge of implementing strategy as well as creating it?*

Margaret has gained the trust of the chairs to run things as she sees fit and is starting to make some progress and develop rapport with the broad Penmarche teams. These efforts consume much of her time, and the research program is suffering from a lack of full attention, understaffing and equipment challenges.

Ruth is a clear thinker and good collaborator with physicians. She has built an extremely effective administrative team to support her while she tackles her own responsibilities as well as large portions of the president role's. Lacks a title to support all her efforts.

When he'd shared his notes, Mark had agreed with him that there were too many nebulous roles needing redefinition. Jay had to restructure the group and clearly define each role – bucket list item #1, Standard #9. However, this responsibility hadn't fallen on him accidentally since Phil had made no attempt to deny leaving certain loose ends for the next CEO to handle. *Approach Walter and Brent for collaborative solution,* he scribbled in the margin of this section of notes. He needed to initiate a courageous conversation – Standard #8 – if he wanted to secure his team of leaders in positions where they could succeed as soon as possible and establish their roles before his time and ability to do so ran out.

Bucket list item #2 was for Jay to develop a culture of "yes" or volunteering discretionary effort constantly – Standard #3. This extended beyond his team and organization to payers, partners and the community. Mark reminded Jay of the 5th Standard, encouraging him to connect with the leaders of each and dig into and leverage the many separate realities that stymied future growth. He'd made a note that the first step to doing this was to *revive negotiations with ND Health and get an agreement in place.*

To accomplish this and the many other items in his outline, he would lead by example – Standard #4 – to mend old relationships and build new ones. The first and most critical one was with Sherman, which had improved significantly over the past few years but still wasn't the valued partner it could be. Jay, having a close tie with Sherman, knew the huge opportunity lost by allowing that bond to falter. He also hoped to strengthen external relationships as well to avoid missing opportunities for additional philanthropy and improvements to the health of the children in their region. Now equipped with the CEO mantle, he could devote time to building the bridges that would span the gaps in their capacity for care.

The third goal on his list was easy in concept but difficult in execution. Jay believed that bringing everyone back to their "why" would aid in combatting the growing burn out problem within the organization, a commonplace in many healthcare institutions. From the custodian to the surgeon, each person played a critical role in the mission and health of children. Jay hoped to rekindle that passion and urge everyone to be in the moment and remember *why* they had wanted to help children. In the fast pace of life, it was too easy to lose focus and let routine replace ambition. They must embrace the gift of care that they were giving children every day.

Jay had long since made a commitment to the 10 Standards of Behavior Mark taught him, honoring and displaying them in every aspect as a leader, or at least trying to. He wasn't perfect, but Mark often reminded him that it wasn't about that as much as it was about progress. And there wasn't anyone who could argue Jay's progress over the years. He had included his personal vows to the Standards in his bucket list, especially to #7 – looking in the mirror and being accountable. If he demonstrated them all consistently in conjunction with the 10th – teaching, coaching and mentoring – then perhaps he truly would be able to execute his substantial yet time-compressed agenda.

Lost in his thoughts, he didn't hear Natalie standing in the doorway, knocking. She entered without his awareness, quietly approaching his desk. She was surprised by how familiar the office felt despite being much larger and furnished with more expensive looking furniture.

"Knock, knock," she said, softly, trying not to startle him.

"Hmm?" he looked up, taking a moment to switch gears. "Oh, Natalie! Hi!"

"Hey. Everything ok? I knocked for a while…"

"Oh, yeah," he waved his hand in dismissal. "Just reviewing my plan of attack."

They both chuckled before Natalie asked, "Surely, they aren't making you work late on your first day as CEO?"

"What do you mean?" He looked at his watch for the first time since standing in the kitchen that morning. "Holy crap! That can't be the time!"

"Well, I don't know what your watch says, but it's 6:30. I had to stay late to finish a proposal, and when I was on my way out, I saw that you were still here, so I popped in."

"Wow. I had no idea. Thanks for pulling me out of the zone," he joked, standing up and shuffling his papers into a neat stack. "Between getting settled, my meeting schedule, and preparing to hit the ground running, I guess I lost track of time."

"Understandable. Do you want me to wait for you?"

"Sure, if you want to, that would be great. It won't take me but a couple minutes to wrap things up here."

Jay organized his desk, made a few quick notes to organize his thoughts for tomorrow, put his computer to sleep, grabbed his things and followed Natalie out the door, which he locked behind them.

"So, how was the first day, Mr. CEO?" she asked, nudging his side.

"Well, it couldn't have been too bad if you had to drag me away from it!"

Jay and Natalie talked all the way to her car, where they parted ways, promising to schedule another dinner date once they got each other's spouses' availability. As Jay walked over to his car, which was parked in the spot reserved for the CEO, he looked up at the top floor of the building and found his new window. Shaking his head in disbelief, he slid into the driver's seat, started the engine and made his way home.

***

"Well...?" Kathy called out from the kitchen, hearing Jay come through the front door. He placed the package he'd diverted from the side entry to retrieve on the island before setting his things down and kissing Kathy's cheek as she diced up vegetables for dinner.

"Jay…" Kathy coaxed again, craning her neck to find him in the kitchen without having to abandon her task. She heard him open a bottle of wine and grab glasses from the cabinet but did not hear any reply.

"Dr. Greenspan, answer your wife!" she demanded, only half-kidding. "Is everything ok?? How did today go?!"

He walked over to where she stood and placed a glass on the counter next to the cutting board. With an exaggerated motion, he leaned against the counter and took a long swig of his wine. This achieved exactly what he'd hope it would; she put the chopping knife down and pivoted to face him.

"What happened today, Jay? Why aren't you talking?!" she crossed her arms and eyed him suspiciously.

After a few more moments of stalemate, a smile spread across his face. He took another swig, maintaining eye contact with her as he did so. She reached for her glass and took a sip, staring back at him, waiting him out. She knew this game. It was what he did when he'd had a good day and was in a playful mood. Depending on how her day had gone, this could either annoy or amuse her, but it always surprised her that he was continuously willing to gamble on which outcome it would be.

"Dammit, Jay. Just tell me!" she begged at last. Amused.

He laughed and held his glass out towards hers in cheers. She clinked it while rolling her eyes at him, "Why you think that is fun is beyond me…"

He laughed again.

"Aren't you going to ask me how my first day went?" he

inquired with sarcasm. "What kind of wife doesn't do that first thing?"

"Ohhh, I'll tell you what!" Kathy replied in mock frustration, tossing a diced pepper at him.

"Ok, ok," Jay relented, picking up the pepper that had bounced off his forehead onto the floor. "The day went well. Nothing too terribly exciting to report, but it was a good day nonetheless."

"Well, you're home later than I expected, so I guess it's safe to assume you weren't looking for things to do all day."

"Oh no. Definitely not the case," he scoffed. "Definitely not going to be the case at all."

"Oh? Well, that's good." She resumed her chopping, listening intently to him.

"Certainly is! In fact, I'm not sure 10 months will be enough time to put even a dent in my bucket list. There is so much I want to accomplish for the organization, so much change I want to enact to get us to the next level...to make the competition take us more seriously," he confessed, his tone filling with genuine concern.

"I know, honey," she consoled in a tone that matched his. Her concerns varied from his though. She worried he would try to take on too much – an impossible mission – that would result in him feeling as if he'd failed when he had no real chance in the first place.

"I suppose it could be done if I keep up momentum and motivation..." he trailed off, sinking into his thoughts as he often did with opportunity on the horizon. She took another sip of her wine and studied his face.

"Where has Dr. Greenspan gone off to now?" she joked, pretending to search his eyes and the area around him for any trace of the man she was just conversing with.

"I'm here," he assured with a smile. "I'm here."

"Well, good. God knows it took me forever to get you to speak tonight."

He chuckled, still wading in the fog of his bucket list. He pushed off the counter and out of his leaning stance to relocate to the kitchen table where he plopped down harder than he planned.

"Alright, Jay," Kathy said, sensing a thunder cloud in his blue-sky day. "Out with it…"

"Hmm?" He sipped his wine, staring off at nothing over the rim of the glass.

"What's troubling you?"

"Hmm?" he repeated before forcing himself to refocus and return to their conversation.

"I can tell something is bothering you, and I need you to make sure you don't bite off more than you can chew. I know you have so many things you want to tackle, but you may need to prioritize this bucket list of yours. I mean, there's only so much one person can accomplish…"

"No, no. It's nothing like that. I *have* prioritized things already. Mark and I combed through my transition notes then reviewed them multiple times for proper sequence, making sure they contained the Standards of Behavior. Plus, we also spoke on the way home to refine the plan of attack."

"Oh good!" Kathy said, relieved to have Mark to help taper Jay's ambition to more realistic levels.

"Yeah…It's just that…" he hesitated. She waited. "It's just that, well, I'm most concerned about the long hours some of these objectives may require, which means losing time with you." Rubbing the back of his neck, he looked at her, blushing and hopeful.

She scraped the vegetables she'd finished chopping into the pan that awaited their arrival.

"Well, Justin will be off to Alabama in a few weeks, which will officially make us empty-nesters. I'll be able to fend for myself if you need to put in extra time to make the difference you want to make. It's actually the perfect time for you to work long days, if there ever were such a thing." She wiped her hands on the dish towel she'd slung over her shoulder and checked on the progress of the meat in the oven.

"Can you believe that our last kid is college-bound? It feels like yesterday we brought him home from the hospital," Jay remarked. "Just goes to show you...if 18 years can feel like a blink of an eye, imagine how fast these next 10 months will go!" The reality hit him once he said it out loud.

"Yep," she agreed, looking over at him, once again, staring off in the distance. "Alright, so which one are we addressing first, then? Justin leaving home or the time-compression of your bucket list?"

"I guess the bucket list," he selected, standing up to grab the plates she was handing him.

"Ok. Remember that we've lived through worse schedules; between our conflicting service and on-call shifts, the kids, as toddlers, running us ragged, or your liquid ventilation trials...We'll be fine! Plus, we'll have the weekends," she comforted. "Just be sure to keep Thanksgiving and Christmas open, so we can go to the farm with my family."

"Of course, of course," Jay replied, feeling relieved to hear Kathy be so nonchalant about his impending hours. She removed the meat from the oven, letting it sit while she dished out the rice and vegetables onto their plates. When

they eventually sat down to eat, Jay moved the conversation to how her day had gone, refilling her wine and listening to her recount a day in the Emergency Room.

***

Jay, equipped with his refined bucket list and Kathy's
blessing to devote the necessary time to achieve it, dove
head-first into his new role as interim CEO. In an effort to
boost morale and make leadership more accessible again,
he arrived early each morning and spent the first hour of
his day walking the halls, observing his staff in action and
thanking them for their hard work. He wanted to facilitate
discussions and reward positive behaviors and results.

He was careful to smile and engage, purposefully
being in the moment with any interaction, which had
the intended effect of easing tensions that lingered from
past governance. Whenever possible, Jay ate in the cafeteria to show his commitment to creating an approachable,
involved, present leadership. By making himself available,
he began earning trust, which led to receiving important
feedback that he could address and incorporate into his list
of objectives.

When in his office, he began putting things in place
for each of his goals. The rigorous activity of grooming
and prioritizing his bucket list was not a pointless exercise.
With so much to achieve in such a short timeframe, it was
crucial that he maximize his efforts in strategic and calculated steps. A few of his goals were hopeful, fresh ideas,
but the majority were organizational improvements or
repairs to existing issues or processes. Regardless, all were
unachievable as anything other than CEO, and each relied
on the careful cultivation of relationships, whether internal

or external, old or new.

Now that he (temporarily) had the necessary title, he coupled it with his extroverted personality to create an unstoppable force and finally make the changes he'd wanted to make for so long. He set forth towards resuming the stalled negotiations with ND Health. Simultaneously, he increased the voice of the providers by including several doctors and nurses in the weekly meeting of administrative leaders. He used their input to make real decisions, which not only further enhanced morale and trust, it improved the process, giving the organization a more holistic way of thinking. He encouraged everyone to "operate at the top of their licenses." For example, nurses were empowered to act as independently as possible, freeing up the doctors a bit, and administrators were able to make certain decisions without seeking approval from supervisors, speeding up their turnaround and processes.

In the evenings, if he wasn't attending a dinner with the state or local government, he was dining with one of many community agencies, from the March of Dimes to the Union League. At these events he was able to listen to the needs of the community so he could address them and form the necessary bond to become their preferred children's hospital and a trusted voice for the children. It was also at these engagements where he developed a preference for shrimp cocktail over-stuffed mushrooms.

All the elbow-rubbing had the intended effect, allowing Jay to sow the seeds of one of his biggest objectives at the next Dayton Business Round Table event.

"Executing the contract with ND Health has put Maynard on the right path to many other opportunities. We are now able to offer care to children from OH and IN, including the more challenged populations, further realizing our goal of health equity and inclusion," Jay announced clearly and proudly into the small, personal microphone in front of him.

"Combined with our recent efforts to offer culturally sensitive care for the local Amish, Mennonite and Orthodox Jewish populations, we're on the brink of a new Maynard and becoming a friendlier, more collaborative and supportive children's health system. All children deserve equal care! All children belong at Penmarche! And we pride ourselves on our mission to make that a reality right here in our community."

Finished with his summary of progress since the last assembly, Jay turned off his microphone and awaited the usual follow-up questions and comments.

"We have noticed many of your recent efforts and acknowledge the notable change we are seeing within the Maynard organization," Senator Riche stated, leaning into her own microphone. Jay scanned the room, watching the other roundtable attendees nod and mumble words of agreement.

"Thank you, Senator," Jay replied, humbled to be complimented in a room full of some of the state's most powerful and influential people. "Although it is still new, I feel this progress will not only be a lasting transformation but will position Maynard to support the mental health facility the state recently proposed. I believe this to be the next best way for our organization to support the community, and if we can work together with the state to secure financial assistance, I am confident we can provide care to the children and youth of Ohio in a way that has been far too neglected for far too long."

Jay leaned away from the microphone but kept his hands folded on the table and eyes on the senator.

"We have reviewed your in-depth and well thought out proposal and agree that partnering to address the mental health of Ohio's children is critical and long overdue. With that being said, we have drafted our response to your request for financial support. Please review it and come back with any questions or concerns at our next meeting." The senator flashed a smile that Jay would have missed had he blinked. "Moving along to the next item on our agenda..." she said as she flipped a page in her notes and continued the meeting.

Upon the conclusion of business, everyone filtered into the lobby area outside the meeting room where refreshments were being offered. The light blue carpet softened the commotion as people shuffled about the selection of cookies, pastries and coffee. The wallpaper's stripes, otherwise imprisoning, were subdued by a plethora of potted plants, which pocked the area. The light from the meeting room's large wall of windows spilled into the lobby, feeding the greenery and warming the room. As Jay took to networking, he was approached by the senator.

"Jay, thank you for leading this mental health facility effort. It is very near and dear to my heart. The children of this state, of every state, need this type of treatment in the worst way," she recognized.

"Oh, not a problem. It's been something I've wanted to initiate for some time now. I'm just glad to have your ear on it," he admitted, thinking about his father and how so many suffer from mental issues that go unnoticed or untreated due to a lack of knowledge and treatment options or stigmas around asking for help.

"Well, I will do my best to get you what you need to make it happen. In fact, I would be proud to do so. I actually can't think of something better to fund, at least not something that is as important and ignored." The senator smiled and waved to the head of the teachers' union as she walked by. "You know, I will also say that making you CEO was the right move. I've worked with Maynard and the other hospital organizations for a while, and they so rarely have someone leading whose heart is in the right place. I can only hope Walter isn't stupid enough not to give you the job permanently," she sighed at her own words.

"Yeah well, he did tell me I wasn't going to be a candidate, and we both know that Walter isn't one to change his mind...ever!" Jay chuckled, secretly agreeing with her despite knowing the truth of his statement.

"No, he is not! It would do him good to do so on some things though!" she confessed. "But, for now, we'll just focus on getting the project approved and funded."

"I appreciate you advocating for its cause," Jay said, genuinely. "Thank you for allowing me a spot and voice at the round table as well."

"Oh, of course! Not that I really have a choice though, to be fair," she admitted, light-heartedly.

"True, but even so, what's not to like about me anyway?" Jay joked, confident that all the dinners and events had built a relationship he could joke in.

"Well, for starters, you being a Bengals fan is one reason!" she laughed and shrugged her shoulders as if to say there was no rebuttal for such an offense.

"Hey, hey! You're the Steelers fan living in Bengals territory, so *I'm* not the problem here!" Jay retorted, shrugging his shoulders and putting his hands in the air to show that he doesn't make the rules about these things.

"I prefer to think of Ohio as a blended state that leans more towards supporting the Browns, which is a misdemeanor compared to your felony," she quipped back.

"Fair enough," he laughed, shaking his head. "I guess we'll have to agree to ignore that aspect of each other in order to continue working on this project together."

"I think I can do that…" she agreed, sarcastically. "At least until football season starts!"

"Obviously," Jay replied with exaggerated emphasis.

She swatted at the air, smiled then extended for a handshake. He returned the gesture, but his smile faded.

"In all seriousness, Senator, thank you."

"And in all seriousness, you're welcome. The world needs more doctors, hell more people, like you," she declared then moved on to mingle with others.

Jay stayed and networked for the appropriate amount of time before heading home. Once inside the house, he put a to-go box of desserts from the roundtable on the counter for Kathy then headed upstairs where he found her reading in bed.

"Why hello there, stranger," she purred, looking over the rim of her reading glasses at him.

"Hi there, Dr. Greenspan," he said as he loosened his tie and pulled it through his collar.

"How did the roundtable go? Did they comment on the proposal?"

"They did, and I think we might get funding for it. Nicole has a dog in this race too, outside of her advocacy for children," Jay reminded.

"Oh, that's right," Kathy said, remembering the senator's daughter having some mental handicaps.

"Yeah, so I know that if it doesn't get approved, it's not for her lack of trying."

"Well, that's good! One more item to soon check off!"

"Yep! But I'll tell you," he started, sliding into bed next to her. "I could use a night or two off from the dinners and shaking hands and kissing babies."

"I bet! You've been going full steam for months now."

"No other choice," he admitted, taking the book out of her hands. "I still have *some* steam left though."

She smiled and flipped off the light before turning back to her husband and sinking into his embrace.

15

Leadership Goes Viral

As always, Jay fell into a rhythm in his new role. In a few short months he'd managed to boost morale significantly, build solid relationships for Maynard with various state and local entities, establish and determine clear roles for the leadership team that directly reported to him, and strengthen the organization's footprint in the industry by partnering with the large payer in ND Health and other community agencies.

Halfway through his assumed tenure, he was feeling confident about his progress to date and hopeful about the remaining time he had. Being the decision-maker certainly made executing some of his plans much easier. No longer did he have to endure long, drawn out justification periods or navigate the reluctance of previous leadership. He had cultivated a more open-minded "yes" culture that was willing to take a risk for the betterment of the organization and benefit of children's health. He was pleased.

On a particularly cold January day, Jay sat behind his desk, flipping through scores on the latest US News and World Report rankings from December. *These standings sure don't seem to reflect what is important to children,* he thought. *It's pretty obvious that they like the larger hospitals. It's virtually a popularity contest!*

"Jay, did you get the email?" Natalie's voice cut through the silence as she walked across his office to his desk.

"Which one?" he joked, becoming serious when he looked up at her.

"The one from the W.H.O. about COVID-19."

"Oh, no, I haven't seen that one come through yet. Let me check." He clicked open his email, scrolling for a moment before finding the right one, which he quickly skimmed. In that time, 3 more emails came through. "Ok, sounds like it's only a matter of time before this reaches us. We should probably have a meeting to get aligned."

"Yes, the number of cases throughout the world is multiplying daily. What is Maynard's planned response? Do we have one?"

"Well, we have the Incident Command System (ICS). You know, what was developed decades ago to respond to the California wildfires then compounded after 9/11..."

"Yes, yes. That works well for blizzards and Hurricane Sandy and the likes. But those are short-term events. Surely, we will need something additional to support a large infection rate. We simply don't have the capacity for a long-term, massive influx of patients," Natalie exclaimed worriedly, talking out loud more so than to Jay.

"I'll call a meeting. At a minimum, I think we need to consider setting up the ICS because it's so regimented and defines the command-and-control protocols, making all directives uniform from a singular source. But I'll get everyone necessary in a room so we can discuss preparations. It's prudent that we have a consistent and targeted approach to combat this virus...ahead of time," Jay assured her.

"Right, right," Natalie acknowledged. "Let me know if there's anything I can do to help."

"Will do. It's still hard to believe that we're facing a possible pandemic," he admitted.

"I know," she said flatly. "Looks like you have the topic for your next weekly video though," she said, wryly referring to the weekly videos he produced with the PR team, which he used to commend associates who had gone above and beyond the prior week and inform every one of the "goings-on" of Maynard, both upcoming and past. These had become popular as everyone enjoyed the vehicle for the messages they contained. He even used sound effects and music.

They both chuckled before Natalie left, and Jay returned to his work. He sent out a meeting invite to Walter and several other leaders regarding COVID and mobilizing the ICS. He had been closely following the spread of the virus since it first became known and was confident that they needed to prepare for when, not if, it came to Ohio. But unlike a hurricane or blizzard, he was fairly certain that this would affect the entire enterprise, making it a good time to set up an enterprise-wide incident command system (EIC). He hoped Walter would agree.

***

Later that week, Jay walked into his office after getting a fresh cup of coffee from the cafeteria. It was a typical February day in Ohio, grey and cold, and the HVAC unit seemed to kick on continuously to combat it. Jay checked his schedule. Only 9 minutes until his weekly status call with

Walter. *That's not enough time to get started on anything,* he thought, clicking on one of the many homepage articles on the spread of COVID, this one breaking down the infection rate in Italy and China, noting the common denominators and few outliers. *Good thing we had that meeting.*

While Walter worked through his proposed enterprise ICS idea, Jay had pitched it to the leaders from the Business Round Table, calling some important points to attention that the group seemed to seriously consider, especially since the virus had now touched down in the states. Though no one in Ohio had contracted the virus yet, they knew it was inevitable as it was spreading down from New York and across Pennsylvania at a ferocious pace.

Jay read on until his desk phone rang at the top of the hour, startling him out of the article.

"Right on time!" he spoke into the receiver. "Good morning, Walter."

"Good morning, Jay. In addition to our normal agenda, we have a few items from the COVID meeting to discuss as well," Walter informed, using no more emotion or urgency than usual.

Jay ran through their standard list of topics, providing updates to or requesting feedback from Walter, before steering the call to COVID.

"The group and I have conferred, and we would like you to assume the Enterprise ICL role," Walter stated.

Jay snorted. Surely, they weren't serious. He'd just taken on the CEO role, which was keeping him more than busy. Even if he wanted to, he didn't think there were enough hours in the day to take on the added amount of responsibility required from the Incident Command Lead.

"Well, Walter. This wasn't what I was expecting," Jay

began. "But I'm happy to do so."

"Wonderful," said Walter. "We appreciate you accepting. As always, we know you'll get us where we need to go."

The two talked over a few more details before ending their weekly call. As Jay replaced the receiver in its cradle, the HVAC kicked on to usher the cold out once again. Jay opened the top drawer of his desk and withdrew his bucket list, now adorned with checkmarks, countless edits, coffee marks and dog ears. He reviewed the carefully crafted plans, his goals and dreams methodically spelled out in order of priority and likeliness of achievement, and, at the top, added: *Guide Maynard through the global pandemic*.

***

"You did what?!" Mark cried out in disbelief. "Tell me you're joking, Jay."

Jay laughed. He knew Mark would react this way. He always encouraged Jay to think before committing.

"I'm not kidding. Obviously, I'm not crazy if the leadership council proposed it. It's not like I volunteered for the job!" Jay said, becoming slightly defensive at the realization of how insane it sounded for him to take this on.

"Where does this leave your objectives as CEO?" Mark asked in earnest.

"I fully intend to continue implementing the key strategic and cultural initiatives." Jay paused to collect his thoughts. "Look, I get the surprise, but we're talking about a global pandemic here! It's uncharted waters for everyone, so we can't know what will be required of me or what kind of time it will consume."

"Exactly!" exclaimed Mark. "Exactly, Jay! It's uncharted waters for everyone. Not everyone in Maynard, you realize.

Everyone in the entire world! Regardless of the time commitment, there is *no way* this won't overshadow all that you set out to accomplish." Mark's tone was draped in concern. Jay could picture him shaking his head in disapproval.

"I have a lot of confidence in my leadership team. If things get out of hand, I can delegate to them," Jay reassured. "You know I say 'yes' whenever possible. This could be what shows Walter that I'm fit for the permanent CEO position. Ya know?"

"No, I don't know, Jay. Considering that Walter explicitly told you that you were not going to be a candidate for the role no matter what you do or how well you do it, I'm failing to see how you can think otherwise." Mark knew Jay was hopeful to convince Walter that he was the right man for the job, but he also knew that Walter rarely changed course. He hated to see his friend take on this added and incalculable amount of responsibility under false hope.

"It'll be ok. I'm not worried about if I can manage it or not. I'm much more concerned about the actual virus itself," Jay expressed.

"Well, if anyone can handle such a workload, it's you," Mark admitted, still disapproving of the decision. "Just do me one favor..."

"What's that?"

"Please focus only on what you can control. For instance, you cannot control Walter's decision-making. Stop trying to. You've bitten off another massive bite before swallowing the one you were already in the middle of chewing," Mark pointed out, fretfully.

"Fair point." Jay couldn't argue it. He wanted Mark to be more on board, but he understood Mark's apprehension.

"Jay...Focus only on what you can control." He spoke

deliberately, annunciating each word for emphasis. He was used to reining Jay in, but it was always more difficult to do so after Jay had committed to something.

"One of the things that I love about you, Jay, is your passion and excitement. You know that," Mark asserted. "You have so many wonderful ideas, and your heart is in the right place. But you have got to learn to restrain yourself at times. This isn't about success or failure nor is it about leveraging a situation for better compensation. This is about taking on too much to prove yourself worthy of a position you've already been told you cannot obtain, no matter what. You're already proving yourself worthy in what you've accomplished in the past 6 months or so. Hell, you'd proved yourself worthy a while ago, or they wouldn't have even offered you the interim role!"

The words traveled to Jay's ear and hit their mark.

"You're right," Jay confessed. "But I can do this, if not for the permanent role then for myself, the organization and, most importantly, the people of Ohio."

"Fair enough, fair enough. I just don't want to see you get let down again, especially when Walter has been very clear with his intentions."

"Ahh, yes. Good old Standard 9," Jay joked, trying to lighten the mood.

"Hey, I just call them as I see them," Mark retorted in a more relaxed tone. "We all know you're versed in the Standards, especially #3…you just have a tendency to forget that whole 'discretionary' part of the volunteering!"

The two men laughed, chatting a bit longer before ending the call.

Jay exited the highway and drove down the winding road along the river. Beautiful, stone houses lined this stretch of his drive, each with its own slice of neatly manicured landscaping. As the sun went down, porch lights blinked on and silhouettes of children, eagerly awaiting their parent's return from work, appeared in windows. Jay recalled the days when Dan and Jess were little, bouncing outlines in the panes next to the front door. More recently, Justin would have his hands pressed against the glass, peering out for Jay's car. Now, Dan and Jess were out in the working world of adults, and Justin was off at college, beginning his own journey.

What does COVID mean for them? Jay wondered. No one had any way to predict what the next few weeks and months would bring. Jay knew that he had to focus on what he could control, letting go of what he could not. It didn't stop him from hoping though.

16

The Interim CEO &
Not-So-Interim Pandemic

The wind blustered against the hospital as if testing the building's structural integrity. The grey sky that had taken over earlier in the month seemed content in its effect, which was to amplify the chill in the air. Inside, the wind and sky were ignored, replaced by the rush of physicians and staff tending to their patients.

Throughout the hallways and floors, Jay's voice permeated the air with a mix of confidence and concern. His current weekly video had been distributed that morning and was being broadcasted on all the hospital televisions, as usual. After several shout-outs to the week's outstanding associates and routine housekeeping items, the topic shifted to COVID. Somehow, Jay and the PR team had found background music suitable for a pandemic and combined it with graphics to illustrate the importance and uncertainty of the virus they were all now dealing with.

In the video, Jay explained the organization's decision to expand the ICS structure to an enterprise level, emphasizing the gravity and breadth of the situation. He defined the anticipated process for relaying information, which would include a daily email, from him to the entire organization, communicating plans and decisions to all. The video ended with Jay introducing the new Enterprise Incident Command team that he had assembled and thanking everyone for their diligence and cooperation during such uncertain times.

"Until tomorrow…" said a smiling video Jay, the familiar sign-off signaling the production's end. Several clicks could be heard throughout the hospital as departments, sure that their entire staff had seen it, turned off the video that would loop for the next hour until all had received the message. For anyone who missed it, a link was sent via email.

Jay left a small conference room after a meeting about cultural initiatives and rushed back up two floors to a larger one in order to host the first virtual meeting with the complete incident command. Once connected, his face populated the top center box of the Brady Bunch style display of attendees. The newly appointed EIC chief of staff, Nick McNabb, started things off by informing each member of their responsibilities and reporting requirements. Each officer – Safety, Public Information, Liaison, Finance, Logistics, Operations and Planning – made the necessary notes. Walter joined fashionably late to show his support, causing the attendee photo grid to restructure. The physical attendees from Maynard sat watching the screen that projected the virtual meeting for all to see.

"As a result of the rapid spread, Pennsylvania, Ohio and Indiana are planning a coordinated response to stay as ahead of this as possible," Nick went on to inform. "That being said, I feel it is now prudent to meet daily as too much changes too frequently that even one day could mean a whole array of new developments. Will this noon timeslot still work for everyone?" No one objected. "Please feel free to add anything you feel is important," Nick added, handing the floor over to Jay.

"Thanks, Nick. As always, I will keep everyone updated on any communications I have and expect that you all do the same. This is not the time to lose focus or stray from a team mentality. I chose each of you for a reason. I fully trust you to take the initiative to manage your tasks in conjunction with your existing, normal workloads. I also expect that you will communicate any issues or obstacles before they become impacts.

"Remember, we are identifying issues and making rapid decisions, finding our footing as we go. So far, we have run things crisply and effectively, but please don't be afraid to use the resources available. Delegate to the smaller, local COVID response committees. We created them for that purpose." Jay looked at his team of eager, capable associates and noticed the collective apprehension pulsing in the room, like a throbbing injury.

"Thanks, Jay," Nick said. "Let's move through the rest of the command structure now. I'm particularly concerned about the scale and availability of our personal protective equipment (PPE), so let's start with logistics. Brian, the room is yours."

The group progressed diligently through the rest of the agenda, but the mood was dire. They contemplated slowing down elective surgery and limiting access to care. Everyone was concerned about their own safety and that of their families as well as the potential for children to not seek care and become sicker as a result of the fear of the virus. Drawing on the 4th and 5th Standards – modeling desired behaviors and respecting separate realities – Jay decided to give his team a much-needed pep talk at the next pause.

"It's ok to be afraid," he began. "Sometimes, the unknown is scarier than a known threat. There is no way to predict the outcome, so we all need to focus on what we can control. I am confident that, together and following the protocols in place, we can successfully and safely navigate these uncharted waters. I promise to maintain clear, concise, authentic and timely communication in an effort to keep everyone informed and, hopefully, help alleviate fear.

"Stay alert and in the moment. Our jobs are already hectic, our teams faced with challenging and difficult decisions regularly. Trust yourself and your team members the way I trust you all. Maynard is headed for a brighter and better future. This virus doesn't change that. Stay on course and stay focused. You, we, can do this!" He looked to Walter in the bottom left square. "Walter, would you like to share a few words?"

"Thanks, Jay, as a matter of fact I'd like to add something. I want to echo our confidence in all of you. We are very aware of the uncertainty of the situation and want to make sure that you all remember to take some time for yourself as well. This is not a sprint but a marathon. As you all well know, it is important that you take care of yourself, so you can help others, as well as Penmarche, throughout this pandemic. We are here to support your efforts."

After a brief pause that indicated Walter had finished, Jay adjourned the meeting before emotions ran any higher, thanking everyone for their time and efforts. He knew he had to be the lighthouse in the storm, and regardless of how uncomfortable that made him at times, it was part of his job as interim CEO.

He fielded a few directive clarifications that filtered in

afterwards and reiterated his appreciation for everyone involved in the coordinated pandemic response. Walking back to his office, he realized that Walter had shown up to offer his support and confidence – nothing more, nothing less – in his typical, concise manner before silently signing off the meeting. Jay couldn't decide it that was a good or bad thing.

***

True to its adage, March came in like a lion. It seemed that things were changing daily, each week completely different from the last. Jay and his EIC team had done a wonderful job pivoting to the constant developments and rapid evolution of the global pandemic. The anticipated arrival of the March lamb proved fruitless. The lion remained, roaring fiercely, showing no sign of departure. *Maybe the April showers will get rid of it. After all, cats don't like water,* mused Jay as he slid on his face mask, securing it in place by tightening the straps on either side.

Ohio, along with many others, had begun declaring states of emergency, placing restrictions on businesses and citizens. In addition to mask mandates, anyone not considered essential to daily operations was told to stay home. Although a hospital, there were ways for Jay to decrease the amount of people and promote, what was being referred to as, social distancing – encouraging individuals to remain 6 feet apart. He ordered a stop on all elective procedures and sent as many associates as possible home to work remotely.

The EIC rolled out new protocols seemingly every day. The dizzying pace of change was communicated via a necessary daily EIC email from the 'Desk of Jay Greenspan'. Whenever Jay ran into associates in the now near-empty hallways, they thanked him for keeping them well-informed. Additionally, a team of PPE coaches was established to round in the buildings on a regular basis to enforce compliance with the new rules in an effort to allay any outstanding concerns from the staff still tasked with a physical presence in the hospital.

All scheduled meetings we converted to video conferences rather than in-person gatherings, and the call for additional meetings seemed to shoot through the roof. Jay felt as if he was constantly on video, interacting with virtual colleagues that, despite their tenure together, now felt unfamiliar and far away. Similarly, his bucket list sat neglected in his top drawer, simmering on the back burner of the pandemic.

In a rare instance of no scheduled virtual meeting, Jay opened his desk to review his list. Expecting more frustration, he found himself pleasantly surprised by the number of items he'd checked off in the short time since assuming this interim role. The organization was operating smoothly and enjoying more recognition from the increased admittance that resulted from the contract with ND Health and other cultural initiatives. Associate morale had risen to healthy levels after he bridged the gap between leadership and staff communication and decision-making involvement. New or previously stalled programs were gaining traction under the newly established risk-tolerant mentality. And, most importantly, his leadership team had received clearly defined roles that were likely to remain in place long after his interim tenure.

Jay was humbled by the realization of all he'd managed to accomplish. The past 7 months had flown by, and now, with COVID, the last 3 months were sure to do so at an even more accelerated rate. *Only 3 months left*, he thought. He willed himself not to want the permanent CEO position, but he couldn't override his desire. He truly enjoyed being at the helm of things and knew he was good at it. He was well-liked both in and outside the organization, which was how he had achieved so much. *Didn't that count for something?*

"Jay?" his intercom blurted.

"Yes?"

"Your 9:30 has joined early. Did you want me to open the call?"

"No thanks, Annie. I'll hop on now. Thank you!" Jay replied, sliding open the camera shield he had only just closed.

"Senator Riche! Long time, no talk!" Jay greeted, sarcastically.

"I know, right?! That 40 minutes between the Governor's call and this one felt like 4!" she quipped without missing a beat. "It seems like we have an endless stream of meetings these days. COVID sure keeps us busy!"

"It sure does," Jay agreed, more emphatically than intended.

"Well, we can't let it completely take over. What movement has been made on the mental health initiative since our last discussion two weeks ago?"

Jay proceeded to run through the action items, updating the senator on the progress of each, identifying obstacles and mapping out next steps. He refused to let this project get overshadowed by the pandemic, but he knew it would require active effort to maintain momentum. Fortunately, the senator wanted it just as badly as he did, so he wasn't alone in the cause.

***

By Thursday, Jay was prepared for but unsure of what would come from the second of the two bi-weekly Governor's meetings. So much had changed in the 48 hours or so since the previous one held on Tuesday. The number of cases continued to increase, and most, if not all, states had shut down everything deemed non-essential. Schools were no longer holding in-person education, transitioning everything over to remote learning by way of video-hosted virtual classrooms. Many adults suddenly found themselves working from home, replacing travel and meetings with video conferences. It seemed Jay was no longer the only one with days full of virtual interactions.

Jay signed into his meeting, ready to address the need for additional hospital beds as well as field any new needs that may have arisen since Tuesday. The Governor wasted no time getting to his agenda.

"Moving on to the need for approximately 300 beds… Does anyone have a proposed solution?" the Governor asked, hopefully.

Jay, clicking on his flag, indicated that he had a suggestion. No other flags lit up.

"Dr. Greenspan, please proceed."

"Thank you, Governor, and hello everyone. I have given this some thought and am confident that Maynard can support any number of pediatric patients since we own the vast majority of pediatric beds in the state. Fortunately, COVID is not impacting children as much as adults, so the focus needs to be on adding adult beds to support the anticipated increased numbers." Signs of agreement could be seen in the muted faces of the participants.

"Maynard has ample space, both internally and externally, on its property that could be converted to an alternative care site (ACS), relatively easily and with minimal cost. In fact, our rehabilitation gym is not currently being used due to the virus and associated restrictions. We could house a substantial number of adult patients in there alone. Plus, it being on our campus will alleviate the strain of setting up a make-shift facility because we have everything onsite from the necessary PPE and clinicians to a pharmacy." Jay stopped there, waiting for questions, comments or concerns.

"Thank you for taking the time to consider the situation," the Governor commended.

"My pleasure. It's not like I have anything else going on," Jay remarked, sarcastically. When no one reacted, at least not positively, to his comment, he quickly added, "I have some specifics written up for your review, if you're interested."

"That would be very helpful, thank you," accepted the Governor, pleased with Jay's suggestions and ignoring the minor faux pas. "I look forward to the information. Anyone else with a proposal?"

No flags lit up. No other ideas for locations to house additional beds were proposed. Jay felt a sense of pride, being the only one with a proposal in a (virtual) room filled with so many important people. He shrugged off the awkward moment after his attempted joke and absorbed the rest of the topics, noting which required action on his end. When the meeting ended at its scheduled stop time, Jay found he had an hour to himself. No meetings. No deadlines. So, he dug into the mental health project that, in light of school now being taught remotely, was more important than ever for the children. There was no telling what anxieties, depression or other psychological impacts this lockdown would have on the youth.

***

The call came through at 7:00 on a Sunday morning. The Governor's ICL, AJ, informed Jay of their intent to use his proposed location, letting him know to expect the Army Corps of Engineers to contact him to schedule a site visit. Jay assured him that he would get the ball rolling, immediately calling Julie to relay the course of action. Within a few hours from AJ's call, an entire team was dedicated to the initiative.

Julie, who had established her own ICS structure that met twice a day, had little difficulty executing the directive. Understanding the urgency, she had the ACS open by Friday of that same week for the Army Corps to assess and the ability to accept patients finalized the following day. Jay was beyond proud of his team, boasting their accomplishment to anyone who would listen. After all, Julie and her team of 50 talented people had worked in unison to proudly achieve the monumental task of converting a gym into an adult hospital in 5 days! This was not something to take lightly. It needed to be celebrated because it was evidence of the leadership Standards' effectiveness and the potential for success when properly executed.

As May rolled in, it became clear that the ACS would not be needed since Ohio had successfully flattened the curve of infection. However, the efforts were not wasted. Rather, they had proven the power of Maynard's teams and their ability to respond creatively and collaboratively in the face of uncertainty. This strengthened relationships with the other regional hospitals and local and state government. It also served as a reminder of the mission; helping people stay healthy. The ride was far from over, but at least they had successfully avoided a flood of infection.

"I'm on my way home. Did you already eat or have a plan for dinner?" Jay asked Kathy as he pulled out of the hospital parking lot on time for the first night in weeks.

"I hadn't even thought about it yet, honestly," she admitted.

"OK, great! I'd say let's eat out, but nothing is open. Did you want me to stop at the grocery store on my way home?"

"I think some places are doing take out."

"Oh really? If that's the case, do you have a preference?"

"Actually, I was just thinking today that I could go for some Chinese," she suggested.

"I could go for that myself. Call in the order, and I'll swing by and pick it up on my way home," he said.

"Perfect!" Kathy replied.

"See you soon then!" Jay exclaimed, happy to have a night off from his CEO duties. He drove to the Black Orchid in silence, enjoying the peace and quiet of not being needed at the moment.

Pulling into the driveway, his headlights illuminated Kathy making her way around the side of the house. She turned, shielding her eyes, and stopped to wait for him. The two ships, usually passing in the night, pulled into port together, finally able to share a meal, which they set up buffet-style on the counter.

They dished out their portions before heading into the living room, figuring they have enough formalities in their professional lives, eating in front of the tv wouldn't hurt anything. Kathy selected something for them to watch while Jay poked at his lo mein and checked the emails that had come through on his commute, one of which was from Walter.

> Jay,
> Don't read too much into this, but I cannot
> search for a CEO while the Incident Command
> Center is standing, and the pandemic
> continues. I am putting the search on hold
> for the time being. In the meantime, keep us
> heading in the right direction.
> Thanks,
> Walter

He froze, chop sticks midair, noodles hanging out of his mouth.

"What?" Kathy casually asked, noticing the abandonment of Jay's table manners. "Did you eat one of those baby corns you hate again?"

"No...thank god," Jay said as he hurriedly sucked the noodles into his mouth so he could explain. "Look at this," he exclaimed, thrusting the phone into her face, displaying Walter's email.

She read it then shrugged her shoulders, giving him a look that lacked the surprise he'd expected.

"What do you think it means?" he prodded.

She shrugged again. "I don't know. Probably nothing more than what he said – he's putting the search on hold until the pandemic is under control. It makes complete sense, actually. He'd be an idiot to change guard amidst the chaos, not to mention he can't exactly interview candidates while we're all locked down, holding everything virtually."

"True..." Jay acknowledged. However, he couldn't help wondering if it meant something more.

"Jay, he specifically said not to read into it..." Kathy

scolded, knowing all-too-well that he was doing precisely the opposite.

"No, Kathy. He said not to read into it *too much...*" Jay flashed her a roguish smile.

She rolled her eyes and took a bite of her eggroll. Debating the semantics of the email was not an exercise she felt like participating in. He was going to analyze it no matter what she said, and, if she learned one thing from listening to Jay relay years and years of Mark's coaching, it was that she had to focus on what she could control. And Jay's thoughts certainly did not fall into that category.

She fluttered her hand at him, granting him permission to carry on, and unmuted the television. He chuckled and turned his attention to Cillian Murphy's dark expression on the screen, directing his fellow Peaky Blinders in their next power grab.

"I'm turning on the closed captioning," Kathy notified. "Sometimes I can't understand their accents."

"K."

"Try not to read into those words too much either..." advised Kathy, sardonically.

"I promise not to read into them...*too much,*" he agreed with a wink.

Kathy released a quiet exhalation of amusement and finished off her eggroll.

17

Virtual Interactions &
In-person Reflections

Jay received no follow-up on the email from Walter, so he stayed the course as best as he could. The pandemic had stalled more than the candidate search, however. He had been able to check off several of the key items on his bucket list, but some were still half-baked after the pandemic arrived and monopolized the past 4 months.

The transition from in-person to virtual meetings had hampered his ability to adequately forge the necessary relationships and partnerships. Although he liked to consider himself a quick learner, adjusting to and becoming comfortable with video conferences was taking longer than expected. He suspected he was not alone in this as he often watched his colleagues and other meeting attendees struggle with their camera settings or other functionalities that undermined the, already diminished, personal interaction. Nonetheless, he trudged ahead, working towards the conclusion of his objectives.

As interim CEO, and in addition to his role as Enterprise ICL and staying on top of the evolution of COVID, he continued working on the mental health initiative with the state of Ohio, maintained focus on modeling the leadership Standards, and sustained the empowerment of his team leads. When race riots began sprouting up across the country in response to police brutality, Jay knew he had to add *guiding Maynard towards a greater awareness* to his list.

Using the 5th and 6th Standards, he encouraged his team and the entire organization to assess the societal temperature with curiosity rather than judgment. He promoted the benefits of respecting and leveraging separate realities by highlighting different cultures in his weekly videos and making a conscious effort to remove any unintentional derogatory language or expressions from his speech. First, though, he issued a formal response to the racial unrest where he deliberately incorporated each and every Standard, knowing that doing so would provide the best results.

He crafted a statement that was in the moment, authentic and humanistic, advocating for action to provoke a change in the current system through modeled behaviors. He called on everyone in the organization to lead that change by approaching interactions and/or conflicts with curiosity instead of judgment, which would naturally bridge separate realities. He encouraged self-awareness and holding oneself accountable for any contribution to the unrest, small or large, intended or not, as well as having courageous conversations with individuals when faced with disagreement, conflict or misunderstanding.

Jay explained that these were not suggestions but obligations to uphold for the sake of the organization, society and humanity, which he planned to develop throughout

Maynard and the community. Despite the fact that his statement contained a few, minor typos and wasn't reviewed or approved by the Public Relations department prior to distribution, Jay's sentiment largely hit its target and reinforced to his staff that he truly did care.

Jay kept both hands on the wheel as he navigated the responsibilities of a CEO leading a growing organization and those of an enterprise ICL managing responses to a global pandemic. As a leader, he promoted growth and awareness during societal unrest while also focusing on the ideas he wished to bring to fruition before his time, and, thus, ability to do so, was up.

Natalie lightly knocked on the doorframe of Jay's office. He waved her in, finding a stopping point in his work.

"Hi, Jay. I can schedule a meeting to discuss this, but I figured I'd pitch it to you quickly first and let you determine the need for one or not," Natalie said as she sat down onto the edge of one of the chairs offered to guests.

"Alright, whatcha got?" he asked, leaning back, folding his hands behind his head and kicking his feet up onto his desk.

Natalie sat silently and expressionless, looking at him until he decided his lax body language may be the cause of her reluctance to begin. He removed his feet from his desk, placing them on the floor and his hands folded on his desk, leaning forward with attention.

"Thank you," she acknowledged. "As you know, it is critical for us to cultivate partnerships in the other major cities in the surrounding area if we want to expand our capacity for urgent care and meet our need of 10 more facilities with a budget for one."

She paused, so Jay nodded.

"There is a new company, PM Medical, that has 3 urgent care facilities in Indiana, in areas that would be perfect for us, strategically, and I feel that creating a partnership would allow us to spread and scale more rapidly. I would like to explore this opportunity."

She paused again.

"OK, I don't see any reason for you not to. I trust your intuition on these things," Jay affirmed, trying to empower her.

She averted her eyes, looking down at her hands in her lap.

"Did I say something wrong?" Jay asked, genuinely confused by the disappointed reaction she gave.

She inhaled slowly, as if summoning courage, and returned her focus towards him. She exhaled and straightened in the chair. Jay mirrored her, sitting upright, unsure of what would transpire.

"Jay, may I be honest with you?" she began, drawing another deep breath.

"Sure, of course you can," Jay urged, drawing a breath of his own that he, instead, held.

"I'm not entirely comfortable with your leadership style…" she confessed, with a small and very hesitant smile.

Jay blew his breath out in relief, smiling so as to welcome the feedback.

"It's just that…I'm used to over-preparing for an ask and having at least half of my suggestions shot down. I feel like you don't shoot anything down," she elaborated, her hands furiously fidgeting in her lap.

"OK….? Forgive me, but I'm a little confused. I thought that would be a good thing?" he remarked, puzzled by yet interested in her logic.

"Well, having all my ideas approved is great, but it can also feel, at times, that you aren't challenging me." She shifted in her seat as her anxiety lessened. "I appreciate you trusting me and my ability, but if you say yes to everything I pitch, it can seem like you aren't fully engaged or taking me seriously."

Jay considered this. He'd never thought about it that way. He could see her point, although it was not the case. He understood how empowering her without probing for substance could be interpreted as disinterest rather than trust. He asked her to speak freely and offer any other constructive feedback she deemed appropriate, which she obliged. He absorbed her assessment of his leadership and thanked her for having the courage to communicate it with him. They worked through a few ways he could challenge her, helping her better vet her ideas before coming to him with them.

"If it helps, I suppose I could yell at you from time to time, so you feel more comfortable," Jay offered, laughing at his own joke.

"Oh, I don't miss the old culture of being constantly challenged that much, but that certainly would make it feel a bit more familiar!" she replied, laughing as well.

"Ok, so I really do like your idea about partnering with PM Medical and would like you to explore that possibility. Can you please do a little more digging in the benefits and risks of such then schedule a meeting with me to discuss your findings?"

Natalie smiled. "I would be happy to!"

"Great," Jay said, standing up. "And by the way, you've done great work since August. Think of all you've accomplished! You have an incredible knack of knowing when to move and when not to. I'm just going to have to keep staying out of your way whether you like it or not. Now get to work!" he shouted, winking at her as she smiled and turned to leave.

"Thanks, Jay."

"No, thank *you,* Natalie. I look forward to hearing more, my door is always open."

"In that case…" she added, pivoting in the doorway. "Maybe stop propping your feet up in meetings and, well, sit up straight!" She cringed and raised her eyebrows, apologetically.

"Noted." Jay nodded and watched her leave. He was beginning to understand that there was such a thing as too casual, particularly as CEO, and was grateful for the insight.

***

April showers brought May flowers. The spread of COVID slowed, violent reactions to racial tensions had lessened, and Maynard maintained its momentum. Jay continued working on his bucket list, making steady progress amidst the chaos of the job. It seemed that he, and the organization, had found their stride.

Although Jay found himself working long hours, a typical workday beginning at 5:00am and ending at 9:00pm, he thoroughly enjoyed the responsibilities and day-to-day requirements of the CEO role. He began to wonder how much time he had left. Not having heard a word from Walter about resuming the search and the 10-month mark only days away, he was half-soothed and half-concerned by the radio silence.

"Hey, no news is good news…" Mark said, reaching for the cliché after exhausting the hypothetical reasons for

Walter not reaching out. He hated hypotheticals but knew Jay needed to go through them in order to prepare himself for the inevitable news.

"That may be so, but it doesn't make any sense. Tomorrow marks 10 months, and he hasn't said one word to me about the search since he put it on hold last month. And we talk regularly!"

"Jay," Mark said, calmly. "You have to manage your expectations. Walter's silence does not negate his originally communicated intent."

"Ugh! Are you always this level?? You can't tell me you aren't slightly intrigued that I haven't heard a peep from him. Not a peep!" Jay paced back and forth behind the closed door of his office.

"Once again, I'll advise you to tailor your expectations!" Mark snickered. "It's not that I'm level, I just choose to deal in the tangible, manageable aspects of things rather than theoretical scenarios or reasonings."

"God bless Cheryl!" Jay declared, frustrated by Mark's unflappable demeanor.

"God bless my wife is right! But for more reasons than just the one you're implying!" Mark knew his ability to remain even-keeled drove Jay insane, but it was necessary, nonetheless. "Someone has to tether you, Jay, or you'll float away. You're lucky you made it as far as you did without popping."

"I cannot and will not deny how beneficial your leadership Standards have been in guiding me, more purposefully, down the path of success." He stopped pacing. "But *you* cannot deny that a good tailwind is not the reason I landed in this position either." Jay asserted, doing his best not to sound like a kid on a playground saying, *I know you are but what am I?*

"You're right. I, too, cannot and will not deny that." Mark agreed, still unflustered.

"OK then."

"OK then."

There was a break in the conversation while Jay collected himself and Mark waited for him to finish.

"So, what am I supposed to do? Just keep on keepin' on until he decides to fill me in on his plan?" Jay asked, annoyed at the unknown.

"That's all you *can* do. You can only –"

"Control my own actions. Yeah, I know."

"Jay, relax. So far, nothing is off schedule. Obviously, it's unlikely that he'll show up tomorrow with the permanent CEO, but even if he did, he told you 10 months, and it's been 10 months." Mark paused and heard Jay let out a frustrated sigh. "Jay, what is this really about?"

Jay didn't respond right away. Instead, he considered why he was suddenly so frustrated, and with Mark, of all people! After several more moments passed, Jay plopped down onto the couch he'd gotten decades ago, when he received his first office position. It slumped against the window, standing out amongst the rest of the furniture, like Cinderella at the ball after midnight.

"I need more time…" he quietly divulged. "I *want* more time…"

"I can understand that. I think anyone could." Mark did his best to console his friend. Even though Walter had made the terms of this arrangement clear, he couldn't help wanting a different outcome as well.

"I've busted my ass to get things accomplished. It doesn't make sense. I know what Walter said, but…but—"

"But you don't know *why...*" Mark guessed.

"Exactly! I don't know *why* he didn't give me a chance. I've brought us back within budget, boosted morale, and increased our footprint, capacity, and brand by securing a contract with ND Health after years of stalled negotiations, and formed partnerships with other local entities that the previous leadership failed to do. I've forged countless relationships and repaired even more...all in ten months! Ten months, Mark! In the middle of a goddamn pandemic!"

"I'm not sure we will ever know his *why*, Jay. It sure doesn't make sense, especially given all that you *have* achieved in such a short time. And you didn't even touch on half your accomplishments. All I can tell you is that you must try – and now hear me out – try to focus on the things you can control because this, this will drive you nuts!"

"You're not kidding," Jay conceded.

"Listen, don't get yourself down. If Walter doesn't see these things, I know others will. They already are! Keep doing your thing. It will pay off no matter what."

"I hope so," Jay mumbled.

"I know so," Mark proclaimed. "I know so."

18

The Long-awaited Verdict & Short-lived Sentence

The 10-month mark came and went. Jay plowed ahead, working to either complete the remaining items on his bucket list or at least secure them in place for future fruition. He made significant headway on the mental health initiative that he and Senator Riche were coordinating efforts on. His enterprise ICL role's intensity had decreased but was nowhere near being unnecessary. The leadership team was running like a well-oiled machine and collaborating nicely between departments.

Jay's days were still packed with action items, stacked neatly in collated documents on his desk, filed in email folders or saved in a voicemail box that swelled to capacity. To accomplish each item in order of priority and stay on top of the constant inundation of requests, he developed a routine, a plan of attack, typically around 3:00 am when his brain woke him out of a dead sleep, like an excited child on the eve of a trip to Disney World. Still, he was always energized, ready to tackle another day.

He managed to push aside his feelings of impatience

and frustration about the uncertainty of his tenure, focusing only on what he was able to control. Any time they threatened to boil over, Mark talked him down and reminded him of his mission.

The one-year anniversary of his interim role was on the horizon when a meeting invitation with Walter wedged its way onto his calendar. Jay hurriedly clicked open the invitation and found no agenda attached.

That's unusual, he thought. Fighting the instinct to call Mark and hypothesize over Walter's intent, he accepted the meeting and forced himself to stick with the day's plan. About 30 minutes later, he had a short break between tasks, which was just enough time for his mind to wander down the road of possibilities.

He thought of all the action items in progress, wondering whether he'd be able to usher them to the finish line. Talks of the upcoming school year were taking place, and the Governor had requested his support in ensuring a safe path for educating Ohio's students. Would he remain an involved consultant? With the threat of COVID wanning and states shifting towards reopening, would the CEO search resume? How much time would that leave him?

Shut up, Jay! he chided himself. *You'll find out in less than a week.*

He succeeded in shutting down his untethered thoughts several more times throughout the day before finally succumbing to them on his ride home.

"Hey, Mark. I got a meeting invite from Walter today…"

***

Jay joined the virtual meeting early after testing his camera and computer audio despite experiencing no issues warranting such measures. He did his best to relax his mind from drifting from possibility to possibility. Jay took a final deep breath as Walter's face appeared on the screen. He looked serious, but that wasn't much of a departure from his regular expression.

"Hi, Jay. Thank you for joining the call," Walter said.

"Of course," Jay replied, hoping to sound nonchalant.

"How are things in Ohio? I hear it's been unusually warm up there, recently."

Walter wasn't one for small talk, and it added to Jay's angst.

"Oh, it's not been too bad, but I'm in the hospital all day, so I can escape it," he said, wishing Walter would get to the point of the call. The sudden interest in niceties was excruciating!

Walter adjusted in his seat, better centering himself in the camera's frame. Jay sat still, frozen in anticipation.

"Ok, well I promised you almost 13 months ago that you would be the interim CEO for 10 months while we conducted an external search for a permanent replacement," Walter recapped.

Yes, yes, and...? Jay urged silently.

"Other than having to delay things slightly due to COVID and all, I plan to make good on that promise. I wanted to let you know that I have chosen an individual for the role, and he will be starting next month." Walter delivered the news without emotion, studying Jay's face to gauge his reaction. They both looked into the camera, likely trying to evaluate the other. After several moments of silence, Walter leaned in, folding his hands onto his desk.

"I'll give you a moment to let that sink in and collect your thoughts, but it is important that you know how pleased we all are with your performance over the past year. You have done a tremendous job. You exceeded everyone's expectations, including, I suspect, even your own."

Jay felt like he was in a fog, hearing Mark's advice ricochet off the many questions that filled his head. *Be graceful in rejection. Thank him for the opportunity.* He forced himself to smile into the camera.

"I have seen you grow in so many ways. You have been, and will remain, a very important part of all we do," Walter added, prodding Jay to show any reaction other than the manufactured smile he'd managed to summon.

"I bet you're wondering what you could have done to secure the permanent position."

Jay tilted his head and shrugged slightly, acknowledging the accuracy of Walter's assumption.

"The answer is nothing. There was nothing you could do. We were intent on hiring outside of the institution, for which we have good reason. You did a fantastic job. Maynard is at a crossroads and in need of a fresh perspective." Walter sat back and decided to wait for Jay to fully absorb the news and react.

"I understand," Jay managed.

"I promised you that I would take care of you when this interim role ended, which is a promise I also intend to make good on," Walter assured.

"Thank you. I appreciate that," Jay replied, emerging from the shock. "What are your thoughts on that?"

"Well, I think it would be ideal for you to transition Brian, our new CEO, for a few months, showing him the ropes and bringing him up to speed on all the things in progress before taking a much-needed, well-deserved 6-month sabbatical. I'm sure you have a list of things you'd like to do if you were afforded the time…Maynard wants to give that to you," Walter announced, confident in the path he'd laid out.

I do have a list like that, Jay agreed. *But I don't need time away to complete it!*

Walter watched Jay for any inclination of how he felt, seeing facial expressions and body language that suggested confusion mixed with disappointment, surprise and attention.

"After the break, we want you to return and plan to find a role for you that will continue to fuel your passion. If we aren't able to find that role, I promise to give you a generous retirement, so you can move on as you see fit." Walter saw something flash in Jay's eyes. "But Jay…I really hope you'll stay with us," Walter added, sincerely.

Jay nodded, the artificial smile still in place. Walter was out of information and unsure what to say.

"Would you like to share some thoughts, or would you prefer to take some time and connect with me later?" Walter asked in a tone that was softer than Jay had ever heard him use.

"I would, if you don't mind, like some time. I just need a moment to gather myself," Jay admitted, thankfully. He'd known this day was coming, and had, in fact, anticipated it coming much sooner. He knew he shouldn't be disappointed, that this was the plan from the beginning, but that hadn't stopped him from hoping. *I guess Dad was right,* he thought. *You can't change them by marrying them.* Now, he understood what his father had meant when he warned him all those years ago. Sometimes, no matter what you do or how much you give, the outcome is the same.

Mark's words then echoed in his head. *Focus on what*

you can control and accept the outcome of decisions you cannot influence. A calmness flooded Jay, and he knew he had to listen to the advice of the two men who had most influenced his decisions and guided him through uncertainty.

Throughout his time in the interim role, he'd set out to accomplish as many items as possible, knowing he would have to pass the baton at some point. He and Mark had spoken countless times about tempering his expectations and truly believing Walter's intentions he'd revealed on Day 1. He thought he had done a good job staying focused on the tasks rather than changing the outcome. However, sitting opposite Walter at this moment, Jay realized he really had been unconsciously campaigning for the permanent role the whole time.

Despite feeling like he'd been inside his own head for an eternity, only several moments had actually passed before Jay composed his thoughts to respond.

"Thanks, Walter," he started, signaling he was ready to resume the conversation. "You know that I wanted this role the instant you presented me with the opportunity, and I've loved every minute of it since. It's truly been an honor to have led this organization for the past year."

Walter flashed a soft smile and briefly broke eye contact, acknowledging the disappointment that Jay was feeling.

"However, I will continue to serve Maynard by helping to transition Brian into the role. I cannot thank you enough for trusting me with this responsibility. I'd be lying, though, if I told you I wasn't hoping for more time, at least, to solidify the things I've been working towards over the past 13 months."

"I can understand that. You've set a lot of promising

things in motion," Walter validated.

"Yes, but you have been direct with me in all decisions, particularly this one, and I appreciate that. It didn't stop me from hoping, but that's on me," Jay said, trying to lighten the mood.

"I can understand that as well."

"I'll work with Brian until he is comfortable and see if we can't continue to work towards accomplishing my goals." Jay smiled more genuinely now.

"Thank you, Jay. I can't stress enough how pleased we are with the job you've done. I know it might not all make sense right now, but I feel this is the best path forward for Maynard. Take some more time to collect your thoughts, and we'll circle back in the next week or so to discuss in more detail."

"That works for me," Jay said, happy for the call to end, which it did after Walter thanked Jay once more.

Jay signed off the meeting, saved his work, straightened his desk, and grabbed his keys and phone. As he reached for the light switch, he paused, looking around his office, the place where his dream job had played out. With a huff comprised of disbelief and disappointment, he flipped off the switch and pulled the locked door shut behind him.

At the end of the hallway, the elevator yawned open, and Jay stepped inside. The ground floor button illuminated, and Jay went down and walked to his car to head home early for the first time in 13 months.

***

As word spread through the hospital, Jay was overwhelmed by the collective reaction of anger about the new CEO's arrival the following month. He received text messages and phone calls from so many of the leaders on his team expressing their disapproval of and frustration with Walter's decision and his execution.

"So, there was no word about anything on the 10-month marked, supposed end of the role? And not even after a year in it? Then BAM!? That's just not ok! You've been doing a great job! We all love you as CEO! What the hell is his reason for not making you it permanently?" Julie demanded, echoing the emotions of Natalie, Hannah and the others at the table.

Jay knew he couldn't agree with them out loud. That would undermine the organization, Walter and Brian, as well as Jay's own professionalism. He'd learned a long time ago that even complacently listening to complaints encouraged bad behavioral practices and diminished his leadership persona. Plus, he was on stage, sitting at a table in the cafeteria amidst the current gossip of which he was the focus.

"Well, I'm not sure I have an answer for you," Jay laughed. "But to be fair, Walter *did* tell everyone, including me, that this was going to be the case. So, as frustrating as it may be, it really isn't a surprise, and I trust Walter's judgment and intentions. I'm sure Brian will be just as good, if not better, as CEO of Maynard." Jay had practiced this response so many times with Mark since his meeting with Walter that even he was inclined to believe the words. Regardless, he sold the sentiment well, towing the company line because that truly was best for his team.

Mark had reinforced what Jay already knew; as CEO, everyone would take cues from his behavioral response to formulate their own reactions to the situation. If he displayed his dissatisfaction and disappointment with the situation, his team was likely to follow suit. And since the decision was not going to change, it was crucial for the team to be on board with their new leader. Jay knew he needed to find his authentic voice in order to model for others how best to support Brian and the organization during the transition. It only served to help if he earnestly guided the team towards acceptance while finding his own way there in private. In truth, doing so was likely to help him get there faster.

With Brian coming on in only a few short weeks, Jay worked on preparing for the transition, gathering documents, writing summaries and planning introductions for the impending handover. His days were no longer filled with responsibilities and ideas. He was now getting home for dinner most nights, which was one part of the transition that he liked.

One evening, Jay had beaten Kathy home. Grabbing a beer, he placed the corn he had just finished shucking on a plate on the counter and began preparing chicken for the grill. The baked potatoes were nestled in their tin foil inside the oven, already cooking, when Kathy walked in.

"Hey there," she said, still not used to him being home before bedtime.

"Hey, how was your day?" He leaned his cheek towards her kiss to avoid touching her with his chicken-covered hands.

"Not too bad. Hectic but nothing unmanageable," she replied. "What's left to do for dinner? What can I get started?"

"Nothing. I've got it all taken care of. Figured you could use a break." He rinsed the knife then placed it in the sink, washing his hands afterwards. "Why don't you change into something more comfortable? By then, dinner should be just about ready."

"Can't argue with that," she accepted and made her way upstairs.

A short while later, she came downstairs in a pair of old, worn-to-comfort running shorts and over-sized T-shirt, having traded her scrubs for civilian attire. Jay was coming in from the deck with a platter of chicken and corn, hot off the grill.

"Do you want another beer, or would you prefer a glass of wine?" Kathy called from the refrigerator.

"I'll stick with beer for now. It's too warm for wine."

"Speak for yourself," she said, pouring herself a glass of chilled white wine and cracking a beer open for him. "Do you want a glass?"

"Nah, beer in glasses is for CEOs," he joked.

"Ahh, thanks for clearing that up." She smirked, realizing how nice it was to have her husband back.

The breeze filtered through the open windows surrounding the breakfast nook that housed the kitchen table, gently lifting the napkins from their place without relocating them. The sun had begun to set, but it was still bright enough to eat without needing additional lighting. The smell of freshly cut grass from the landscaping their neighbors had done that afternoon mixed with the BBQ dinner they were sitting down to eat.

Jay placed the platter of corn and chicken in the center of the table and went to pull the baked potatoes out of the oven. Before Kathy settled into her chair, she brought over plates, silverware and the necessary condiments for their meal.

"Man, it's so nice to eat at home again. That's one thing I definitely missed," Jay confessed. "Everyone thinks that being wined and dined is where it's at, but I'll tell you, that gets old really fast."

"I believe it," Kathy said as she lightly buttered her ear of corn. "So, Brian starts on Monday. Are you ready for that?"

"As ready as I can be. I've summarized all the on-going projects and compiled a list of suggested meetings and action items. That's about all I can do until he's here. The rest will just be guiding him through the processes and introductions, I suppose."

"Pretty much. I wonder what he's like."

"What do you mean?"

"Well, I just wonder what makes him Walter's candidate of choice, is all. I hope he knows how big the shoes are that he has to fill. Outside of all you've done for Maynard, you're pretty well-liked there. I can't imagine him being welcomed in with open arms when most aren't pleased with the decision."

"Yeah, I do think that will be his biggest obstacle, initially. No matter how much I promote it or assure everyone that I'm ok with it all, they seem unwilling to accept it."

"Honestly, I can't blame them." Kathy remarked, cutting another bite of chicken while Jay unwrapped and began preparing his potato. "Plus, COVID isn't exactly over, and they're predicting a surge in the fall. I can't say this is a great time to bring in a new CEO..."

"Did you grab the butter?" he asked, hoping to change the subject.

"Oh, oops. Sorry," Kathy replied, moving to retrieve it for him.

"No, no. I wasn't asking so you'd get it. I just wanted to make sure I wasn't simply not seeing it in front of my face the way I do many other things, according to you." He winked at her then went to the fridge.

"What's that casserole in there?" Kathy asked, taking a slow sip of her wine.

"Oh, that?" Jay started to laugh. "Natalie."

"Really? She sent another one?" Kathy chuckled, shaking her head.

"Yep. I keep reminding her that I didn't *die*, I just didn't get the job."

They both laughed, knowing that was Natalie's way of taking care of Jay since changing the situation wasn't an option. She figured the least she could do was make sure he was eating.

"She's a good friend," Kathy smiled. "She has checked in with me almost daily to see how you're really holding up."

"Well, what are you telling her that she keeps sending me home with casseroles?!" Jay asked rhetorically while reaching for the salt.

"I tell her you're doing fine! I mean, we all know you're upset about it, but you really are doing a good job of hiding it, so I guess she just wants to make sure you aren't in the wrong stage of grief," Kathy expressed, eyeing Jay's bite of potato, heaping with all the fixings.

"What?" Jay asked, stopping the fork in front of his mouth. "What are you looking at?"

"Hmm?" Kathy deflected, digging into her corn to excuse her from any elaboration.

"I see," Jay said in mock-offense, dropping the fork back down to his plate. "I know I've put on some pounds over the past year. You can admit it, I'm aware. But there's only so much I can do when there's a dinner or lunch meeting almost every day," he defended, justifying himself.

"I didn't say anything!" she proclaimed, raising her hands in innocence then her glass in cheers. "Plus, you can only focus on what you can control. Isn't that right?" She winked, playfully, unbothered by a few added pounds. "You haven't even gone up a size in clothing or anything. Relax, I'm just teasing you!"

"I'm sure," Jay said skeptically, rolling his eyes impishly to show he wasn't offended.

They finished dinner and did the dishes together before settling on the couch to watch their show, both equally satisfied to have re-established their routine.

After watching two episodes, they made their way upstairs to go to bed. Kathy brushed her teeth while Jay got undressed. As he passed the full-length mirror on the way into the bathroom, he stopped to assess his reflection. He noticed for the first time that his hair, what was left of it, had greyed significantly over the past year and fine wrinkles now appeared around his eyes.

Maybe the job was more stressful than I realized, he thought, leaning in for a closer look. Then, turning sideways, he got confirmation that his weight gain wasn't terribly noticeable but was noticeable, nonetheless.

"Well, with the extra time I now have again, I guess I'll be able to get back to the gym more often," he announced.

"Hmm?" Kathy said, half-listening as she walked by to return her hairbrush to her vanity.

"Nothing," Jay mumbled.

"What a nice night," Kathy sighed contentedly on her way out of the bathroom. "We even have time for some fun," she remarked slyly, slapping his butt playfully.

Jay didn't need any more reassurance than that. He

leapt into bed like an excited puppy and lifted the covers for her with a grin.

19

The New CEO & Lack of Standards

Walter had flown up from Texas for Brian's first day. It was the first visit he'd made in months due to the pandemic. He planned to formally introduce Brian to the team, sit in on a few meetings, then head back mid-week. Jay had arrived earlier than usual that morning in a successful attempt at beating both Brian and Walter in. He sat in the vacant office next to the CEO's that contained a desk, chair, bookshelf and seating for visitors. Boxes of Jay's personal belongings and files sat stacked in the corner. The room felt bare without personalization, amplifying the change.

At 7:00, Jay heard Brian enter the neighboring office and begin settling himself in. Jay waited, expecting him to come introduce himself or peek in to see if the room was occupied, at a minimum. At 7:30, Walter joined Brian to inquire about his morning agenda, which, according to Jay's eavesdropping, was filled with meetings.

That's weird, Jay thought, checking his email for calendar invites but seeing none. He then heard Walter leave, heading down the hall in the opposite direction from the offices. *Nice to see you again, too, Walter.* But, as quickly as this sarcastic thought entered his mind, Mark's voice interrupted it. *My thinking drives my behavior,* he corrected himself, knowing that negative thoughts sprout negative behaviors. *Ugh, why does it have to be so hard sometimes to live the Standards on a moment-to-moment basis?* And with that, Jay decided to do what he believed any new CEO should and walked next door to introduce himself.

Brian sat at the desk that was formerly Jay's, typing away at the keyboard.

"Knock, knock," Jay said from the threshold. Brian looked up and stood to shake hands.

"Jay Greenspan. I wanted to introduce myself, welcome you to Maynard and let you know that I'm here to assist you with the transition," Jay informed more cheerfully than he intended or felt.

"Thanks, I appreciate that. Once I get my arms around some of the stuff Walter gave me to get started on, I will reach out if I have any questions." He sat back down, which told Jay that he wasn't interested in more than an introduction at that point.

"Alright, well I'll let you get settled. I'm in the office next door if you need me."

"Thanks again," Brian said, returning to his typing.

Sure, my pleasure, Jay thought to himself, walking out of the office and back into the spare, unaware that he'd allowed another negative thought to creep in. He spent the next hour wrapping up some remaining loose ends and replying to the emails from colleagues and contacts expressing various reactions to the transition that ranged from well-wishes in future endeavors to downright outrage at, what some deemed, an unfair and illogical decision. Regardless, the outpouring support reinforced to him that he had, in fact, done a good job and left a positive mark in a short time.

Lunch time approached, and Jay did not want to eat in the cafeteria, pretending to be content. He checked his calendar and, finding no meetings scheduled, called Mark to see if he wanted to grab lunch.

When they entered, they found the diner at pandemic capacity, which meant only 50% of the tables were allowed to be in use at a time. Their favorite booth was unavailable, so they stood in the small entrance that was hardly suited to be called such, eyeing the tables and counter seats for signs of turnover. The remains of freshly baked pies rotated slowly in their glass cases on the counter, the coffee maker gurgled and hissed like a runner with a cramp, and the waitresses, unaccustomed to the new guidelines, hustled about, serving and clearing dishes as the need arose.

"Sheesh," Jay remarked, rubbing the back of his neck while he silently debated waiting.

"It's not usually this busy," Mark noted.

"I'm not aware of anything going on nearby. It's not like there are any conventions in town right now. Don't get me wrong, I'm happy they have business; I just wish we could give them ours because man, am I hungry!" Jay said, placing a hand on his stomach for emphasis.

"Well, it doesn't look like we'll be eating anytime soon if we stay here."

Jay exhaled a frustrated sigh. *Great,* he thought, cynically. *I wonder what else today will bring.* He rolled his eyes at the notion.

"Let's just find somewhere else to go," he suggested. "It

doesn't look like they have much left anyway." He nodded his head towards the crossed-out specials on the chalkboard and picked over bakery cases.

"Yeah, good point. There's a whole bunch of stuff along this street, so let's just walk and see what we find. I'm sure there's some place that hasn't shut down and isn't at capacity," Mark suggested.

They turned to leave after giving their regular waitress a wave and smile that both wished her luck and let her know they weren't unhappy about the wait. She returned an exasperated yet cheerful expression as she maneuvered with her hands full around the newly installed plexiglass dividers between the tables.

"Well, that was certainly unexpected," Jay exclaimed, catching the door before it slammed shut, which made its bell jingle more than usual. They walked down the sidewalk towards the other restaurants that lined this section of the city, dodging other people doing the same.

Eventually, the two settled on a Greek restaurant that resembled the diner in size but not crowd. They were led to a small, blue booth in the corner, which, unlike the diner, did not have a window or plexiglass divider beside it. The hostess, who Jay assumed was likely either the owner or related to the owner based on her Greek features and age, handed them menus with the daily specials clipped on top and walked away. A few minutes later, she returned with two waters and a notepad to take their orders.

Jay began to bring Mark up to speed on how his day had gone before they'd met at the diner, pausing only to gauge Mark's reaction at various intervals.

"So then, Walter showed up, walked into Brian's office, spent, I don't know, 20 minutes max in there, reviewing

Brian's meeting schedule then left."

"He didn't stop into your office at all?" Mark asked, rhetorically, sipping his water and raising his eyebrows in surprise. "Well, rather than assuming something negative, let's assume that it was a simple oversight because he was rushing to get somewhere else."

Jay threw his hands up and let them land loudly on the table. "Are you kidding me, Mark? We both know that neither of them is going about this the right way. Forget about professionalism and all that obvious stuff, and just think about how illogical it is to transition in without any feedback, guidance, or briefing from the person who previously held that position! Who, might I add, is more than happy to assist! It's ridiculous!"

"Well, I can't say that I'm surprised by Walter's behavior or your reaction to it." Mark paused a moment to craft his words carefully and give Jay time to calm down a bit. "Hmm, how do I put this…"

"Bluntly, please! There's no need for anything else," Jay prodded.

"OK then. Walter's behavior makes sense to him and yet, for some reason, you expect it to make sense to you. When it doesn't, you become judgmental and stop being curious. Remember, this is all about separate realities. If you want to better understand why he does what he does, you simply need to ask him. Period."

Jay looked at Mark and considered his point.

"Yeah, I suppose you're right. I know you are…" he confessed, rubbing the back of his neck while he thought more about it. "If I'm honest, it's not really even Walter that's bothering me. I mean, I'm used to Walter being Walter. He's usually very…focused." Jay attempted to laugh away his frustration. "But now that you mention it, I can see how I become judgmental and move away from curiosity in that regard."

A momentary, quiet contemplation fell over Jay. "What I am certainly curious about, though, is why Brian wouldn't want any input from me. OK, so he doesn't feel he needs my help, fine. But don't you think it would help to at least include me in meetings, even just to listen in?"

"Jay, there you go again, making stuff up!" Mark cautioned. "You don't know that he doesn't want your help, so stop torturing yourself over it."

Jay stared off into the distance over Mark's shoulder. "But here's the thing, Mark," he said in a less frustrated, more defeated tone. "If he chooses to do this alone, without any of my help in the beginning, there's no way the transition can go smoothly, at least not with the team, and I don't want that for Maynard. In fact, I busted my ass for over a year to get rid of that type of mentality!"

The hostess reappeared, now in a waitress role, to deliver their lunches. She set the plates down on the table and paused to give them a moment to think of anything else they might need. When neither asked for anything, she told them to enjoy their meals in a gruff tone that offered no other option and walked off.

"You can't always have it your way, Jay, as you well know," Mark continued, shaking pepper onto his fries. "And as frustrating as it may be, Brian's behavior is not in your control any more than the results that come from it. All you can do is demonstrate the behavior you wish to see in others. Everyone knows what type of leader you are and what you've accomplished in such a short time. Just look at all the emails and texts you've gotten since the news broke about Brian coming in as CEO…"

Jay waggled his head back and forth because there was no arguing that. "Hell, I'm still getting casseroles!" They both laughed at this, which served to sufficiently lighten the mood.

"Seriously, though. Rather than hypothesizing about his intentions and worrying about the potential impacts of his actions, why not have a courageous conversation with him?" Mark proposed in between bites of his gyro.

Jay nodded with a mouthful, acknowledging the suggestion. "That's not a bad idea. It worked well with Phil, and I could gain a lot from doing so. Thanks. I think I'll try that, actually." He wiped his face, indicating he was finished eating as well as signaling that he was ready to move on, both in conversation and in his role.

"Glad to see you're still working on employing the Standards," Mark admitted.

"It's about progress, not perfection." Jay winked and grabbed his phone to check the email he'd just heard come in. He read it to himself then out loud to Mark.

> Jay,
> I had hoped to meet with you this morning but was running late to a meeting, which then threw the rest of my day off schedule. I'd like to get aligned with you on Brian's transition now that he's started. My calendar is up to date. Please send me an invite for a 30-minute call this week.
> Thanks,
> Walter

Jay looked up from his phone at Mark, who was calmly chewing.

"Don't even say anything," Jay conceded. Mark smiled and wiped his mouth with his napkin. "Not one word!" Jay held his hand up and slid his phone into pocket.

Mark laughed then Jay did too, adding, "Well, still! How was I supposed to know he was late to a meeting? Anyone would have made the same assumption I made!" Mark stopped laughing and went to comment, but Jay put his hand back up.

"Not a word! I know what you're going to say, and whether I like it or not, you're right," Jay admitted, rolling his eyes in playful surrender. Mark put his hands up to show innocence and winked at Jay.

Shortly thereafter, they finished their food, enjoying it regardless of the command to do so. They split and paid the check and made their way to leave. As they stepped out onto the sidewalk, the waitress/hostess/possible owner demanded that they have a good rest of their day, which was enough motivation to make that precisely what Jay intended to do.

***

Brian accepted the meeting invite Jay extended, and the two met later that week. As a result of their conversation, Jay learned that Brian's reality was, indeed, much different and that his own extroverted, action-oriented style had caused him to become impatient with Brian's reserved, lead-from-behind approach, creating negative judgment about his intentions. After speaking with him, he realized that Brian did care about continuing the improvement of the organization as well as hearing Jay's input. He just needed to engage others in his own way, at his own pace.

It turned out that Brian was actually a pretty decent guy,

and Jay wished he'd approached him sooner. *Mark does always say that courageous conversations need to occur in a timely manner,* he thought, admonishing himself. *Curiosity truly is so much more productive than judgment.*

***

As the days turned into weeks, Jay still received emails from the team, preferring to go to him before Brian or professing their continued disappointment that he was no longer the CEO. He responded to both in kind, now with sincerity, encouraging them to give the new guy a chance to settle in, thanking them for being his advocates, and painting a bright picture of Maynard's future under Brian.

He began receiving other emails that contained opportunities pitched by senders hoping for his interest. He knew most were automated, but the few that had come to him, personally, contained plausible options that captured his attention. Of course, he fully intended to accept the responsibility of remaining involved with the plans for the mental health facility he'd started with the state and Senator Riche. This was somewhat cemented for him by the senator's refusal to work with anyone else at Maynard on it, though. She'd grown to appreciate Jay's approach, which balanced her rough edges during the planning phases. Needless to say, those rough edges helped Jay advocate for the purpose. But that position wasn't full-time, nor was it a long-term solution, so he still needed to consider other possibilities.

A headhunter had proposed several viable options, such as Department Chair of several smaller programs and strategist for a pharmaceutical company, the former being the more interesting of them. He'd also considered assuming the role of assisting the lieutenant Governor for the state of

Ohio, but it being a full-time volunteer position meant he also had to weigh its long-term sustainability. There were several enticing opportunities to return to research, as well as a handful to teach residents. He was also still being kept busy by the enterprise ICL position, and, as predicted, the fall surge was coming to fruition.

Another, more creative idea that had been proposed to him was becoming a *permanent* interim CEO, moving from hospital to hospital to improve their leadership and processes before transitioning in a permanent candidate and heading on to the next. Furthermore, Brian had made it clear that he and Walter wanted him to remain at Maynard and assume a key, strategic position within the organization that they were in the process of searching for.

Jay wasn't lacking options. If anything, he had too many to choose from. Between the sabbatical and retirement package, he knew he'd be alright, financially, but since finances had never been a driver for him, he wanted to select the option that would best allow him to help either an entire organization or leadership team within one. It didn't matter because, at the end of the day, he would be helping children heal and/or stay healthy. And that *did* matter.

"These all sound like great options, Jay! I think you'd enjoy each of them for different reasons," Mark exclaimed in support.

"Yes, I agree. There are definitely some good possibilities in the bunch. I wish I could do a bit of each, honestly," Jay said, only half-joking.

"Wouldn't that be ideal?"

Jay leaned back in his temporary chair and kicked his feet up onto his temporary desk with the phone perched on his shoulder. Neither said anything for a moment.

"I know I'll be ok, that's not my concern. I just want to make sure that whatever I choose is fulfilling of my mission to help children stay healthy," Jay professed.

"I have no doubt you'll be ok and continue to fulfill your mission, make no mistake about that," Mark announced. "As you know because this is probably the 100th time I've said it over the past several years; focus on what you can control and accept the outcomes you can't...and lead with curiosity, not judgment!"

Jay smiled. "You're exactly right, just as you were the other 99 times."

"So, then. It's really quite simple, if you ask me."

"Oh yeah? Simple, you say?" Jay laughed, waiting for Mark to break it down for him.

"Yep, it's very simple," Mark said with mirrored insouciance. "Which of the available opportunities do you want to make your next 'yes'?"

ACKNOWLEDGMENTS

I was honored, and very humbled, when Mark Sasscer called me to see if I would be willing to write a leadership book for his friend, Jay Greenspan. I have such a respect for Mark and his work that I didn't hesitate to hear their idea to see if I could execute it properly. Listening to them relay Jay's journey and understanding their goals for the leadership book they wanted to write, I knew, right away, that I wanted to be a part of it. However, I also knew that they had something more special than "just another book on how to be a great leader." They had a story to tell.

I have loved every minute and aspect of writing their story and will be forever thankful to the two of them for trusting me and the process. Although many of the events within took place, Jay allowed me the creative freedom to build a fictional world around them to deliver his message in the manner that, I felt, was best suited. If he hadn't trusted me, this could have been "just another leadership book" on the shelves. Thank you, Jay. Thank you, Mark. Your friendship is inspirational. - *Lauren*

Mark Sasscer's book *'Accountability NOW!'* and my subsequent friendship with the author gave me the foundation to plaster all of my learning experiences into a usable framework. Every interaction, success and failure can be tied to the Standards discussed within his book.

When I was offered the interim CEO position for a year, I knew those Standards had both catapulted me to the opportunity and afforded me the roadmap to navigate the role. I wanted to share that experience with you. I thank Mark for that gift, as well as my colleagues, friends, and, of course, my family, for all of the learning experiences.

I also knew that writing a book that is, hopefully, both a good read with a message required a team. Though I write scientific literature, Mark encouraged the importance of my story then connected me with his friend, Lauren, who had the writing talent to pull it off. What a great team! The process has been fun, and I hope you enjoy reading this as much as we have enjoyed writing it.

Most importantly, I'd like to thank the many nurses and therapists that have toiled tirelessly by the bedside with me, helping, encouraging, coaching, and coaxing me all along to be my best. Of course, the deepest gratitude goes to the babies that have been under my care for the last 4 decades, and their caring parents and family members that want only one thing: good health and a pathway home. *– Jay*

Jay Greenspan MD, MBA has spent over 4 decades as a neonatologist and leader in pediatrics. He was an interim Health System CEO from August 2019 - September 2020 and is now the Professor and Chair Emeritus of Pediatrics at the Sidney Kimmel Medical College at Thomas Jefferson University. He remains

an active researcher with over 150 publications, including his work on liquid ventilation, and presents his work internationally. He has received numerous awards, including the National Neonatal Education Award from the American Academic of Pediatrics, the Lifetime Achievement Award from the Philadelphia Business Journal and the Roosevelt Award for Service to Humanity and Elaine Whitelaw Volunteer Service Award from the March of Dimes. Most recently, he was the Enterprise Incident Commander for an institution's COVID response and the Chief Medical Officer for the Philadelphia COVID response team. He is currently a Co-Director of Hot Topics in Neonatology, the large neonatal conference in Washington DC.

Jay and Kathy live just outside of Philadelphia as do Dan and Jess, his beloved mother, Reva, and his two siblings, Karen and David. Justin is a sophomore at Alabama University. Most of Kathy's brothers live near Youngstown, Ohio while Kathy's father, Roger, lives on a farm in Grove City, Pennsylvania and hosts the very large Nasci clan every holiday.

Jay has devoted his career to giving every baby the best chance at a healthy life. He is thankful for all of his colleagues and the many healthcare providers that have dedicated their lives to this same effort, the March of Dimes for their beautiful mission, and the many essential workers that have guided us through the COVID pandemic. Additionally, he encourages all of us to work to resolve the persisting pandemic of inequity and racism.

Since establishing LeadQuest Consulting over 25 years ago, **Mark Sasscer** has devoted his time and energy to helping senior executives improve business results by changing the way they lead and shape organizational culture. Through Mark's unique style of teaching and coaching, executives of many of the world's most successful companies and institutions have gained a deeper understanding of the impact that their behaviors have on relationships, organizational culture, and performance results.

Among his credentials, Mark published his first book entitled The Change Agent in 2006 and published his second book, *Accountability NOW! Living the Ten Principles of Personal Leadership,* in 2010. View him on LinkedIn and at Leadquestconsulting.com.

Mark currently splits his time between the Eastern Shore of Maryland and Phoenix, Arizona with his wife, Cheryl.

TESTIMONIALS

"*Mae Jemison once said, 'Never limit yourself because of others' limited imagination; never limit others because of your own limited imagination.' This quote reminds me of what Dr. Jay Greenspan does every single day. He is that leader, neonatologist, husband, father, teammate, mentor, and friend who never limits others in doing what they do best. Prized for being an all-around compassionate person, Dr. Greenspan cultivates the best in all of us while fostering collaboration, no matter the circumstances. Whether COVID-19, social injustice, a baby fighting for life, or someone who just experienced their darkest period, he provides us all with the will to go beyond, do better, and be better than imaginable. He has inspired me to be a better human being in this lifetime and for that, I am eternally grateful.*"

– Cindy Bo, a former colleague and senior Manager, Ellen P. Gabriel Fellow, Healthcare, Mergers & Acquisitions, Deloitte

"Jay came into my life when a positive outlook and sense of humor were what I needed most. At the time, I didn't know he was a neonatologist, I just thought he ran a hospital. He was so approachable and kind. Being the mother of a child with cerebral palsy, I found that refreshing, and he became a comfort zone. The more I worked with him, the more inspired I became. Jay's work and outlook inspires me to be a better mother and stronger leader in the healthcare industry. His ability to see the potential and good in life is what makes him stand out amongst his peers. Jay is the type of leader and physician that reinforces the need to support our first responders. I'm lucky to know him. **"**

– Delaware State Senator Nicole Poore

"How do you put into words the gratitude and love you have for someone who took your lifeless, near-death, critically-ill newborn baby and gave her not only a chance at life but the opportunity to become the astonishing woman she is today? On the night Adrianna was born, I first met Jay as the lead doctor in a clinical trial that could possibly save her life. That night, Jay meant many things to me but mainly faith, hope and gratitude; Faith that Jay would make the right decisions, hope that he could save my baby's life, and gratitude for the years he dedicated to research, trying to save babies like my Adrianna.

"Over the years I have been blessed to not only develop a relationship with Jay as a patient's parent and as a neonatal intensive care nurse but, most importantly, as a friend. He is truly an empathetic, loving, caring and dedicated *person inside and out. We are blessed to have had him in our lives for the past 26 years.* **99**

– Toni Mancini, mother of Adrianna and RN at CHOP Newborn Care at Pennsylvania Hospital

1989 - Tom (far left), Marla, and Jay (far right)

1990 - (from left to right) Tom, Jay, and Marla in the New York Times

1994 - Baby Adrianna

1994 - Toni holding Adrianna for the first time.

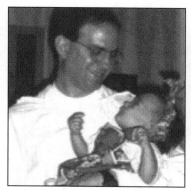

1995 - Jay and Adrianna

1999 - Toni and Adrianna

2019 - Justin, Jess, and Dan Greenspan

2019 - Dan, Justin, Kathy, Jay, and Jess Greenspan

2009 - The Nasci Family - Roger Nasci (center), Kathy (second in from the right)

2019 - Delaware Senator Nicole Poore and Jay

2018 - Jay and Adrianna

2020 - Jay and part of his team

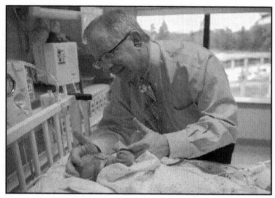

2019 - Dr. Jay Greenspan

ABOUT THE AUTHOR

 **Lauren Mix** has spent over a decade as a performance analyst for power generation facilities throughout the US. She is considered an industry SME on compliance and statistical analysis and has worked with some of the largest energy companies in the country, including Dominion and Duke Energy.

She has also edited over 15 professional books and co-authored *Enterprise Agility in Healthcare* that was published by Taylor & Francis Group in 2018. *Breathing Liquid* is her debut novel.

Lauren enjoys traveling and spending time with her husband, Patrick, and daughter, Mallory. She lives on a farm in southern New Hampshire.

View her on LinkedIn or at LMEditingServices.com.